In the black void all around them, the stars seemed to be sweeping past at merry-go-round speed.

Clinging perilously to the handrails outside the hatch, Tom and Bud managed to brace themselves while they attached the rockets to the rim. Then, holding their reaction pistols, they triggered off a series of short bursts.

Gradually the whirling space station slowed to a halt...

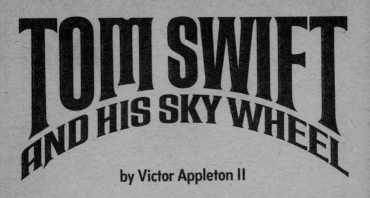

TOM SWIFT AND HIS SKY WHEEL

by Victor Appleton II

Illustrated by Tony Tallarico

Original title: Tom Swift & His Outpost in Space

tempo
books

GROSSET & DUNLAP
A FILMWAYS COMPANY
Publishers • New York

CONTENTS

CONTENTS

ILLUSTRATIONS

TOM SWIFT
AND HIS SKY WHEEL

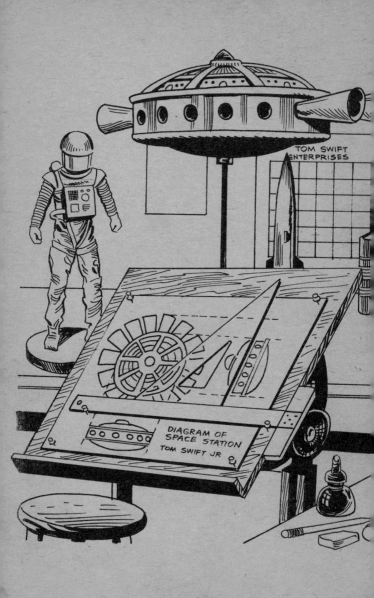

TOM SWIFT
ENTERPRISES

DIAGRAM OF
SPACE STATION

TOM SWIFT JR

CHAPTER 1

DANGER IN THE SKY

"DON'T TRY IT, Tom! We'll blow up!" warned Bud Barclay as his friend, Tom Swift, sent the great silver-winged *Sky Queen* nosing higher and higher into the stratosphere.

"Relax, Bud. This ship can take it," replied the tall, blond young scientist. He kept his deep-set blue eyes focused on the instrument panel.

The altimeter needle showed they were at a height of 85,000 feet—more than sixteen miles up in the purplish black sky.

It was midday and Tom was flying the huge jet plane as high as he dared, in order to test out his latest invention. This was a solar battery, to be charged by the unshielded radiation of the sun.

During the trip Bud had been intently watching the differential pressure gauge. The dark-haired young copilot knew that the pressurized plane was being subjected to a terrific bursting strain as the air outside grew thinner and thinner.

Still the eighteen-year-old inventor kept the ship in a steady climb. Bud frowned. "Don't say I didn't warn you!" he muttered nervously. "If this crate blows up in our faces, we won't even—"

He broke off as the plane gave a violent lurch. There was a groan of tortured metal and both boys were nearly flung out of their seats.

"What hit us? A meteor?" Bud gasped.

"Turbulent area," Tom replied, as the giant craft shuddered from stem to stern.

It turned and twisted wildly in the buffeting winds. Together, the boys fought to bring the plane under control.

"We'd better take her downstairs," Tom decided.

Throttling back on the jet engines to reduce the forward thrust, he began guiding the ship earthward in wide, spiral turns. Tom had great faith in the atomic-powered craft, which was capable of vertical climb or descent. The huge three-decker *Sky Queen*, a completely equipped flying laboratory, had been Tom's first major invention.

Several miles down, the ship reached a safe region of calm air. Tom flipped a switch, pouring power into the jet lifters. Instantly the plane leveled off and seemed to hang suspended in the stratosphere.

The flying companions stared at each other in silent relief. "Listen, chum, don't scare me like that." Bud grinned. "My arteries can't take it."

"Sorry." Tom smiled back. "You know we're apt to run into those ghost winds almost anywhere up here."

"When they blow at two hundred miles an hour, that's when *I* blow!" Bud announced firmly. "Do you suppose this crate is still in one piece?"

"I'd better make sure."

Tom checked a number of gauges, then went off to inspect various pressure points in other compartments. As he returned to report that the *Sky Queen* had sustained no damage, he heard Bud exclaim:

"Jumpin' sky ghosts! What's that at ten o'clock?"

Glancing to the portside, Tom saw a large, silvery balloon floating some distance away.

"Must be a weather balloon." Tom's eyes narrowed. "But I'm not so sure."

Bud glanced at him curiously. "What are you driving at, skipper?"

Tom raised a pair of binoculars and trained them on the balloon before replying. "That box attached to the balloon—it doesn't look like the usual type of radiosonde for sending weather signals. Let's get a closer look."

Easing off on the jet lifters, Bud sent the ship gliding forward. Then he banked in a sharp spiral that brought the *Sky Queen* close to the object. The balloon veered and fluttered in the rush of the plane's air stream, but Bud finally maneuvered the Flying Lab to within twenty yards of it.

Again Tom studied the object as Bud held the

ship steady with the jet lifters. "How about it?" asked the copilot.

"It's no weather balloon, that's sure."

Bud focused his own binoculars on the strange device, then lowered them with a puzzled expression. "You're right. But what is it?"

"Bud, that balloon *may* be rigged for some kind of solar-battery test."

"*What!*" Bud exchanged startled glances with the young inventor.

"It's only a guess. But the equipment on the surface of the box certainly looks that way."

"Roarin' rockets, that means someone else may get the jump on Swift Enterprises before you put *your* model on the market!"

Tom shrugged ruefully. "There's no law against competition."

"Who do you suppose sent it up?"

"Search me." Tom settled back at the controls. "Well, whoever he is, I wish him luck."

The giant bag was rising slowly—floating toward the upper levels of the stratosphere. Then, without warning, the balloon burst, spattering parts of the fabric over Tom's plane.

The instrument box plummeted downward, but a moment later a small parachute opened to float it gently back to earth.

"Hey, let's go after it!" urged Bud excitedly. "Maybe we can find out whether your hunch is right!"

Tom shook his head. "The persons making the experiment are probably tracing the balloon by its signals. They'll be all set to retrieve the box when it lands. And after all, it's *their* experiment."

"Guess you're right," Bud murmured in a disappointed voice. "Where to now?" he added, as Tom sent the *Sky Queen* zooming upward in a steep climb.

"Back upstairs for another check on our own experiment," the young inventor replied.

"Just make sure you don't steer us into that shimmy area again." Bud chuckled. "I'll take those fast numbers on a regular dance floor."

Soon the altimeter needle was approaching the 85,000-feet mark again. By this time, the giant jet plane had traveled a long way from the turbulent area, and the air remained still and calm.

Tom set the ship on automatic stabilizer, then said to his copilot, "Keep an eye on things. I'll go topside and take a reading."

Mounting a short steel ladder, Tom climbed into the astrodome. This was a transparent blister above and behind the pilot's compartment. It was used for observation and navigating on long flights.

Tom's new solar battery had been mounted in an aperture in the dome for exposure to the rays of the sun. At high altitudes the rays were more powerful than in the denser air blanket surrounding the earth. Wires from the battery were connected to a voltmeter and other electrical instruments.

When the young inventor returned to the flight deck, his face wore a disappointed frown.

"Anything wrong?" Bud inquired.

"The voltmeter reading is way down," muttered Tom thoughtfully, running his fingers through his blond crew cut.

"What does that mean?"

"That the battery's efficiency for storing electricity will have to be improved. In other words, the battery will take a charge but won't hold it properly. I'll have to try some other method."

"Maybe you should send up a trial balloon like those other fellows," Bud suggested.

Tom grinned. "We'll go one better and send up an experimental rocket. I think that the best place to power solar batteries is beyond the atmosphere."

"I don't get it," Bud said in a puzzled voice. "How could you go into production? You couldn't send up a new rocket every time—"

Suddenly the copilot's voice trailed off and he stared at his friend. The full meaning of Tom's words had just sunk in.

"Look, genius boy, you aren't thinking of setting up a space station to manufacture your batteries!"

Tom nodded. "Exactly. Dad and I have been talking for a long time about building a space station. We're both convinced that it's practical."

He was about to jot down an equation that had just occurred to him when Bud yelled:

"Tom! A missile's coming straight at us!"

CHAPTER 2

THE GORILLA MAN

AS THE STRANGE yellow-nosed object hurtled toward the *Sky Queen,* Tom went into action. With a frantic lunge, he grabbed the controls and slammed the throttle wide open.

The plane dived like a thunderbolt. Almost in the same instant, the missile whizzed overhead in free flight. Tom pulled the *Sky Queen* out of the dive gradually, then steadied her with the jet lifters.

Bud gulped in ashen-faced relief. "Good work, Tom. Whew! I thought we were goners! Say, that *was* a guided missile, wasn't it?"

"I think so," Tom agreed. "All I could see for sure was the bright-yellow warhead."

Bud mopped his forehead nervously. "Boy, this hunk of sky is really crowded today." Then he managed a grin. "Guess we should have got our reservation in earlier."

Tom frowned. "What I'd like to know is whether that missile was aimed at us deliberately."

"You and me both! I wonder who could have launched it?"

"I don't know, but we'll find out." Tom switched on the radio.

As he waited for the set to warm up, he pondered the mystery of the strange projectile. Was there any connection between it and the bursting balloon? And had the *Sky Queen* been a deliberate target? If so, it was not the first time for such an assault.

After perfecting the Flying Lab, Tom had been attacked in it by rocket missiles, forcing him to fight a ruthless group of enemy agents. Another had been aimed at him recently while he was drilling for molten iron at the South Pole with his atomic earth blaster.

A sputter of static from the radio brought Tom back to the present. He quickly made contact with his base, where a special crew was monitoring his flight by radar.

"Did you pick up an extra blip on the scope just now?" he asked.

"We sure did, Tom. What happened?"

Tom explained, then said, "Try to remember the arc of that blip and track the missile if you can. And have the communications office flash my father. I'd like to speak to him."

"Roger!"

A moment later the voice of the elder Swift came

through. "What's up, son? Any luck with your solar battery?"

"It needs improvement," Tom reported. "But that's not what I called about, Dad. We just brushed wings with a guided missile."

"What!"

"I know it sounds crazy, but it actually happened. I thought you might call Washington and find out if the government has a record of the launching."

"Good idea," Mr. Swift agreed. "The source certainly should be traced. This is dangerous business."

After exchanging a few more remarks with his father, Tom signed off. He and Bud carried out some further tests on the solar battery, then flew back to Swift Enterprises. This was the sprawling experimental station where Tom and his father developed their inventions. The old Swift Construction Company, founded by Mr. Swift, adjoined it.

The Enterprise plant covered a four-mile-square enclosure, crisscrossed by airstrips. Its flat modern buildings gleamed in the early spring afternoon sun.

After landing the *Sky Queen*, Tom turned it over to field mechanics for berthing in its underground hangar. Then the boys headed for the main building, where Tom and his father shared a roomy, private office.

Miss Trent, their efficient secretary, greeted Tom and Bud with a smile. "Mr. Swift asked to see you both as soon as you got back."

With Bud at his heels, Tom hurried into the

private office. The room was large and bright and appropriately furnished with modern furniture. On a long, polished table stood a huge relief globe of the earth and a replica of the planet Mars, as well as scale models of Tom's major inventions.

Mr. Swift, a tall, well-built man of forty, looked up from his desk. There was a close resemblance between the world-renowned inventor and his brilliant son. They had similar, sharply defined features and the same keen blue eyes. Tom stood an inch higher than his father and was lankier.

"Any news yet on that guided missile?" Tom asked eagerly.

"We just had a reply from Washington. There's no report, either public or private, of any such missile being launched."

Bud gave a low whistle. "Then there must be something fishy going on!"

Mr. Swift nodded. "No question about it. That near hit on the *Sky Queen* was no accident. Tom, I suggest that you tighten up all security precautions on your battery project."

"All right. But what about the government—is it going to make a search?"

"That may not be necessary," his father replied. "Your ground technicians seem to have the missile's trail pretty well plotted."

"What a break!" exclaimed Tom, as Bud gave a whoop of triumph.

"They're waiting for you boys now in Ames' office," Mr. Swift added.

"Come on. Let's go, Bud!" Tom said.

Harlan Ames was head of the Security Department at Swift Enterprises. When the boys arrived at his office, they found the slender, dark-eyed man talking to Hank Sterling and Arvid Hanson.

Sterling, the blond, square-jawed chief engineer of Swift Enterprises' patternmaking division, was in charge of the special technicians working with Tom on his solar-battery tests. Hanson, an expert craftsman and Tom's chief modelmaker, was also assigned to the project.

"How about it, Hank—did you pinpoint the spot where the missile landed?" Tom asked.

"We think that it came down somewhere northwest of Rabbit Lake," replied the engineer. "Arv was on the tracking scope."

Hanson pointed to a location on a large map which was spread out before them on a table.

"The computer gave us the speed and course of the missile," he explained. "By projecting beyond the point where it went out of range of our tracking equipment, we figure that the missile must have landed about here."

"That's wooded country, isn't it?" Bud asked.

"In some places," Ames said. "There's a State Police post about ten miles from there if we want help in organizing a ground search."

"Let's try from the air first," Tom suggested. "We'll take the heliplane."

Ames was unable to leave the plant, but asked Phil Radnor, head of the security police, to accompany Tom and Bud.

Riding in a plant police car, they drove to a small hangar at the north end of the property, where the heliplane was housed.

This recent invention of Tom's was a combination airplane and helicopter. Vertical lift for take-off or hovering was supplied by pulse jet rotors. For normal flight, after the ship became air-borne, these rotors folded into the fuselage and the ship operated as a conventional jet plane.

Soon the party was winging its way toward Rabbit Lake. Beyond this body of water, the terrain was rugged and strewn with patches of timber and brush.

For almost an hour they flew back and forth over the area which Hanson had indicated on the map. Tom skimmed slowly along at treetop height while the others scanned the ground with binoculars.

Suddenly Bud gave a shout and pointed downward to the right. Tom swooped low for a better look. In a gully choked with underbrush shone a gleam of bright yellow!

Tom quickly landed the heliplane on a stretch of level ground. The group ran to the edge of the gully and scrambled down to examine their find.

The projectile lay smashed and twisted among

the jagged rocks. If the warhead had carried an explosive charge, it had proved to be a dud.

Nevertheless, Tom waved the others back to a safe distance and alone cautiously disarmed the detonator mechanism. As he scrutinized the device carefully, his companions poked in the wreckage.

"Look for any markings stamped on the metal parts," Phil Radnor advised the others. "They may help us to identify the source."

"Wait a second!" exclaimed Tom. As the others turned to look, they saw him holding a pocket gauge to a small fitting on the detonator.

"Find something?" Bud inquired.

"None of these gadgets are scaled in inches!" Tom exclaimed. "They're all machined to the metric system!"

"You mean they weren't made in this country?" Radnor asked.

"Exactly," Tom replied. "In America and in British countries, calibration of instruments is in inches and gallons. But all other countries use the metric system of measurement. And this angle-of-ascent gauge and fuel cutoff device are calibrated metrically.

The others listened in stunned silence as the full import of Tom's statement sank in. *The persons who had released the missile were evidently foreign agents!*

"We'd better find that launching site and do it pronto!" Hank Sterling said.

Suddenly Tom experienced an uncanny feeling that they were being spied upon. He whirled around just in time to see a man peering out from among the trees at the opposite rim of the narrow gully.

It was a face so terrifying that Tom felt a chill of fear!

"Someone's watching us!" he warned the others, but by then the man had disappeared from view.

Tom dashed up the slope to investigate, his friends following. The tangled undergrowth slowed their ascent. By the time Tom and his companions reached the upper bank of the gully, the man was nowhere in sight. Although the searchers fanned out quickly and combed the nearby woods, they found no trace of the mysterious observer.

"Wonder who he was?" Hanson asked, as they gathered to talk things over.

"As far as I'm concerned," Tom said with a wry grin, "you can call him the Gorilla!"

"How come?" asked Bud.

"Because that's just what he looked like. Heavy shoulders, bushy hair and eyebrows, and a big undershot jaw. He seemed to have long arms like a gorilla's, too."

"Sounds like a cousin of Frankenstein's monster!" Bud said with a shudder.

Turning to Radnor, Tom asked, "Ever run across anyone like that in our subversive files?"

The security officer shook his head. "Not that I can recall offhand. But I'll check with the FBI."

"Whoever he is, I'm certain the Gorilla knows something about that bomb," Tom declared.

Since it was late afternoon, Tom decided that there was little hope of locating the missile's launching site before dark. It was several miles away. So, postponing the search until the next day, the group flew back to Swift Enterprises.

When Tom arrived home for dinner that evening, bringing Bud with him, his sister Sandra and another girl were playing records in the spacious living room.

"Hi, Sandy!" he called to the blond, blue-eyed girl who was a year younger than her brother. "Hello, Phyl!"

Phyllis Newton, a pretty brunette, was the daughter of Ned Newton, long-time friend and associate of Tom Swift Sr. Uncle Ned, as Tom called him, although he was not a relative, now headed the old Swift Construction Company.

"Goodness, you boys had a narrow escape this afternoon," said Phyl, after Bud had greeted them.

"Yes, tell us about the missile," Sandy begged.

After her brother gave a straightforward report of the missile, Bud told of Tom's glimpse of the gorilla man.

Phyl shivered. "How awful!"

"He might make unpleasant company, but I'd like to find him," Tom declared.

"Maybe we ought to take Sandy and Phyl along tomorrow when we look for him," Bud teased, with a wink at Tom. "In fact, I wouldn't be surprised if the Gorilla came skulking around here tonight."

"Stop it! You're scaring us to death!" Sandy said, laughing.

Soon she disappeared to help her mother with dinner and presently everyone sat down to eat. Mrs. Swift, who liked to cook and prided herself on several special dishes, was a dainty, sweet-faced woman. Though she tried not to worry about her family's exploits, she found it hard not to do so. Her husband and son were always encountering some hair-raising adventures, and Sandy, who enjoyed test-piloting small Swift-manufactured planes, was somewhat of a daredevil.

"Um, nothing like your chicken pies, Mrs. Swift," Bud complimented her.

After dinner, when they all settled down in the cheerful living room, Sandy asked, "Seriously, Tom, do you suppose there's any chance of your tracing that gorilla man?"

"I'll say this much," her brother replied. "I'm sure that he's part of the missile plot and we haven't seen the last of him."

The words were hardly out of Tom's mouth when a loud buzzing growl sounded through the house.

"The alarm system!" exclaimed Bud, jumping up from his chair.

The girls looked at each other and Phyl murmured, "Oh, I wonder if that's the Gorilla!"

The Swift residence was protected by a magnetic

field. Anyone disturbing this field, unknowingly touched off the alarm, unless provided with a deactivator mechanism. The Swifts and their close friends wore wrist watches with neutralizer coils.

"We'll soon know," said Tom grimly, getting up from his chair. "It may be just an innocent caller," he added, seeing the look of concern on his mother's face.

As Tom strode to the front door, steps sounded on the porch and the doorbell rang. Tom glanced up at the warning dial above the front door. The needle had swung around violently, indicating that the visitor carried metal—possibly a weapon!

Tom pressed a light switch and peered through the small one-way glass aperture in the door. In the yellow glow of light outside stood a uniformed policeman.

Relieved, Tom opened the door. He started to greet the officer pleasantly but was interrupted tersely.

"Are you Tom Swift Jr.?"

"That's right."

"Then take this." He thrust an official-looking document into Tom's hand. "It's a subpoena ordering you to appear before Judge Grover tomorrow to answer charges of malicious destruction of property!"

CHAPTER 3

A COURT BATTLE

THE NEWS about the summons served on Tom Swift appeared in the morning newspaper, and the Shopton court was packed by the time the Swift family and Bud arrived. Flash bulbs popped as they entered the municipal building, but Tom declined to make a statement to inquiring reporters.

Although the case was scheduled for one thirty, the court docket was so crowded that by midafternoon the case still had not been called. Tom fumed. He had been unable to learn any details of the charge against him.

Bud squirmed and fidgeted. Under his breath he muttered to Tom, "Boy, this is worse than standing by for a rocket take-off!"

Finally Judge Grover intoned, "Case of the Quik Battery Corporation versus Tom Swift Jr. Will the parties please step forward?"

As Tom rose from his seat, a stranger came bustling up the aisle. He was a stocky man, with a florid complexion and bulging eyes that made him look like a bad-tempered bullfrog. As he glanced briefly at Tom in passing, his lips curled in a contemptuous sneer.

"You are the complainant?" inquired Judge Grover, addressing the red-faced man.

"That is correct, Your Honor. I am John York, president of the Quik Battery Corporation. As an attorney and member of the State Bar Association, I will represent my own company in these proceedings."

The judge turned to Tom. "And you are the defendant?"

"Yes, sir."

"Aren't you represented by legal counsel?"

"Our company lawyer is now in Washington," explained Tom. "I didn't feel that it was necessary to call him back on this account, because I'm quite sure that there's been some mistake. I haven't destroyed anyone's property."

"We'll see about that!" snorted John York angrily. "Yesterday my company was making some tests on solar radiation. We sent up a balloon equipped with valuable instruments. Tom Swift deliberately rammed that balloon with his plane and ruined the entire experiment!"

Judge Grover frowned. "Is that correct?" he asked, turning to Tom.

"Definitely not, Your Honor. It's true that I was flying a plane at that time, and I did see the balloon Mr. York is referring to. But it burst of its own accord, just as any radiosonde balloon will do after reaching a high enough altitude."

York sneered sarcastically. "And I suppose you just *happened*, by some strange coincidence, to be around at that particular moment!"

There was a slight titter from the spectators, and Judge Grover rapped for silence. "You will please confine your remarks to the court for the time being, Mr. York. I take it that you are prepared to prove these charges?"

"I am, Your Honor. May I call my first witness?"

"Proceed."

At a nod from York, a tall, thin man came forward and was sworn in. After taking the stand, he identified himself as Frank Haley, a technician employed in the photographic laboratory of the Quik Battery Corporation.

York handed him a sheaf of photographs. "Have you ever seen these pictures before?"

Haley glanced at them briefly. "Yes, sir. I processed these photographs myself. They're shots taken by an aerial camera in the test balloon we sent up yesterday."

"And what do they show?"

"They show Tom Swift's plane, the *Sky Queen*, heading straight toward the camera just before the balloon was rammed."

A buzz of interest and excitement rose from the courtroom. York turned his red, perspiring face triumphantly toward the judge. "If Your Honor will examine these photographs, you will see that there is no doubt whatsoever about the truth of my charge!"

Judge Grover took the photographs and studied them for several moments. When he looked up at Tom, his expression was grave. "Young man, these photographs certainly seem to bear out Mr. York's accusation. Do you still deny the charge?"

"May I see the pictures?" Tom asked.

The judge handed them over, and Tom glanced through them quickly. "The answer is quite simple, Your Honor. When I first saw the balloon, I realized that it was not the ordinary type used for weather signals. So I asked my copilot to steer toward it for a closer look. That's evidently when these pictures were snapped."

York laughed harshly. "Don't think you can squirm out of this!" he said, shaking a fat finger in Tom's face. "These pictures *prove* you rammed my balloon head on!"

Judge Grover rapped his gavel for order, and Tom replied, "If you got your camera back safely and developed these pictures, how can you claim your experiment was ruined?"

This rejoinder seemed to confuse York. He stood, openmouthed, floundering for an answer. "Well, I— I—it's not the camera I'm talking about! It's the other instruments. Practically everything aside from the camera was completely smashed—and all of it was high-priced scientific equipment!"

Suddenly an idea occurred to Tom. With a quick shuffle, he counted the number of photographic prints. Then he looked at the witness. "Mr. Haley, I'm familiar with the type of film which aerial cameras use. And also the number of exposures on each film. There are some prints missing from this one. I'd like to know what happened to the rest of them."

Haley cleared his throat and glanced uncomfortably at his employer. Before he could reply, York snapped at Tom, "What concern is that of yours?"

"I'd like to see them," Tom said evenly. "They may be important evidence. In fact, they might even show that I never rammed your balloon at all."

"Well, you're out of luck," York retorted. "They don't show anything of the kind."

"What *do* they show?"

"Nothing! The rest of the prints were all spoiled."

Judge Grover leaned forward on his elbows. "Does the witness verify that fact?" he asked.

"Yes, sir, I do," replied Haley, nodding hastily.

The judge frowned for a moment, then announced, "I believe you'd better produce those prints, anyhow, Mr. York."

The plaintiff was obviously distressed, his face redder than ever. "But you just heard what the witness stated, Your Honor," he protested.

"Nevertheless, I'm going to insist that they be produced," Judge Grover said firmly. "Without seeing all of the pictures, we have no positive proof of what happened after Tom Swift's plane approached the balloon."

York glared first at the judge, then at Tom. He looked more than ever like an angry bullfrog about to explode. Finally he grumbled in a sullen, ill-tempered voice:

"Oh, very well. I'll produce them if we can still find the negatives in our lab. But I repeat, they show nothing. Since the court chooses to regard them as such important evidence, I may as well drop the charges."

"Suit yourself, Mr. York," the judge said coldly and brought his gavel down. "Case dismissed!"

The courtroom onlookers burst out in a surge of chatter and applause, and once again flash bulbs exploded into brilliance as Tom's family and friends rushed up to congratulate him.

Sandy planted a kiss on her brother's cheek and Bud clapped him on the back, exclaiming, "Why didn't you tell us you were such a legal beagle?"

Mr. Swift shook Tom's hand. "Nice going, son! If you weren't such a first-rate scientist, I'd say you'd missed a legal calling."

"Thanks, Dad."

On the way home Bud kept everyone chuckling with his jokes about York's popeyed reaction when his case started falling apart. But he added, "Just the same, I think that guy would be a good one to stay away from."

"That'll suit me!" said Tom emphatically as he steered the family car through Shopton's late afternoon traffic. Smiling, he added, "We'll be too busy the next few weeks to bother to look him up!"

"Tell me about it," begged Phyl, who had not heard of the latest doings at Enterprises. "Strictly confidential, I know," she took the words from Tom's mouth.

"Do you have some new project in mind, son?" Mrs. Swift inquired a bit anxiously.

"Yes, but don't worry, Mom. It's only in the idea stage so far."

"Well, don't keep us in suspense!" Sandy protested.

"What is it?" asked Phyl.

Tom laughed, then said to Phyl, who could be trusted with any secret, "A space factory where we can manufacture solar batteries."

Phyl gasped. "A space factory!"

"Only a small one," Tom went on. "I'll locate it in an orbit fairly close to the earth, in order to make the job of building it as simple as possible. Say, a little over a thousand miles up. From down here, you could see it racing around the earth like a tiny moon."

"How marvelous!" Phyl exclaimed.

Smiling, Tom's father remarked quietly, "If

you're going to all that trouble, son, why not build a big, more important station?"

"What do you mean, Dad?"

"As you know, I've been hoping for some time that Swift Enterprises could be the first to set up a space station. But I'd like it to be a truly humanitarian project—one designed to serve the interests of all mankind." Mr. Swift paused. "The fact is, Tom, I have a surprise in store for you."

"A surprise? What is it?"

Mr. Swift's eyes twinkled. "You sound just as you did when you were a little boy. And I'll answer you the same way. If I told you what it is, it wouldn't be a surprise any longer. However, I will say this much —a very important group of men is coming to our office tomorrow morning!"

CHAPTER 4

THE MYSTERIOUS WARNING

NO MORE was said about the important visitors, and Tom had to tether his curiosity until the next morning. At nine thirty he and his father were checking blueprints in their private office when the intercom buzzer sounded.

"Mr. Bruce and the other gentlemen you're expecting have just arrived," Miss Trent announced.

"Send them in, please," Mr. Swift replied.

Tom pressed a button, and the drawing board containing the plans and sketches he had been working on slid silently into the wall.

A moment later father and son arose to greet six visitors. Mr. Bruce, who introduced the callers, was a middle-aged man of slim build with a pleasant, confident manner.

"Tom," said his father, "Mr. William Bruce is from the Consolidated Broadcasting Network, and is chairman of this committee of engineers from the major broadcasting companies. They've come to discuss a very important problem with us."

The group took seats, then Mr. Bruce addressed the Swifts. "I'll state our problem at once. As you know, high-frequency-signal coverage in its present form is far from being efficient. Distances are short, requiring many relay stations. Sometimes there's distortion. Also, sunspots or magnetic storms may wreck the broadcast completely.

"In fact," he went on, "any reliable system of short-wave broadcasting over great distances is practically hopeless with our present methods. However, there's one solution to this problem—"

Tom's heart leaped with excitement. He sensed what was coming next.

William Bruce smiled at the eager look in the young inventor's eyes. "As a scientist, you've no doubt guessed what I'm about to propose."

"A space station?" Tom burst out in his enthusiasm.

Bruce nodded. "Exactly. Our committee has come to the conclusion that it's the only way we can hope to lick our broadcasting troubles—that is, by setting up a platform in space to which we can beam radio signals and have them relayed directly back to earth. Naturally, this would be a huge project. But we feel that Swift Enterprises is well fitted to undertake the job."

Tom could hardly contain his elation. Here was a

group of important, hardheaded engineers asking him to expand still further an ambitious project on which he had already set his heart!

"It's a tremendous challenge," he said as he exchanged glances with his father.

Receiving a nod of approval, Tom got up and walked toward his secret workbench which held the plans for the space station.

Meanwhile, Mr. Swift remarked, "Gentlemen, my son has been working on plans for a factory in space. Perhaps you'd like to see them."

Tom came back with several large blueprints which he spread out on his desk. The papers were covered with sketches and mathematical figures.

"My plan," Tom explained, "was to place the station in an orbit 1,075 miles above the earth's surface. But at that altitude it would make one complete revolution around the earth every two hours. And that would not do for broadcasting purposes."

"No," Mr. Bruce agreed, glancing at the sketches. "This station is a very original design," he commented. "Like three spokes in a giant wheel."

"Yes," said Tom. "We could add as many spokes to the hub as we wish. Would one or two be enough for your broadcasting purposes?"

The engineers felt that they would need three for commercial broadcasting.

"And I believe the government would want one," Mr. Swift remarked.

The six visitors plied Tom with questions about

the station which he answered readily. Finally Bruce nodded approvingly and remarked:

"Your plans certainly seem quite sound. From what you've told us, I'm convinced that the station you have in mind is entirely practical. But as you have already said, the station would have to be placed in a much higher orbit."

"Twenty-two thousand miles would be better for broadcasting purposes," Mr. Swift spoke up. "And the station should be in a path directly above the earth's equator, I suppose."

"Yes," said Mr. Bruce. "At that altitude the space station would revolve in its orbit once every twenty-four hours—exactly in time with the earth's rotation. And above the equator it would remain fixed above the same geographical spot at all times, which is what we would need."

"It presents more problems than Tom's original plan," said Mr. Swift.

"We can handle them, Dad," Tom said, smiling.

Then he remarked that it would make the job more expensive to shoot supplies by rocket to such an enormous altitude. But he admitted that from this one station alone, radio or television signals could be relayed to one third of the globe!

"A marvelous accomplishment!" Mr. Bruce said enthusiastically. "Later on, if our project is successful, more stations can be built. In this way, we could ring the earth with a foolproof broadcasting system. Think of it, gentlemen—world-wide television would become a reality! We could pick up TV images anywhere on earth and beam them back to viewers right here in America. That is," he added cautiously, "if all countries consent."

"Well," Tom countered, "even if they don't, at least we'd be able to keep an eye on North and South America."

Mr. Swift remarked wryly that the project would no doubt stir up plenty of trouble from unfriendly countries. "The space station would certainly carry telescopes," he said, "and could detect every warlike move by an enemy. In fact, gentlemen," he concluded, "this will be a very big undertaking from several angles. Therefore I believe the United States Government should be included in the project."

Tom and the broadcasters agreed wholeheartedly and the meeting ended with a promise from the Swifts to take care of this matter. Also, they were to prepare an estimate of what the project would cost the broadcasting companies and submit it.

The visitors had hardly left the office when a red light flashed on the control board of the Swifts' private TV network, consisting of studios in various parts of the country. Tom walked over and flicked on the videophone.

Since the signal was from Florida, he fully expected Kane, the Key West telecaster, to appear. But neither he nor anyone else was visible on the video screen.

Instead, a crudely printed sign came into focus.

Tom gasped and yelled, "Dad! Look!" Staring at them was a message.

Tom Swift: If you attempt to
build a space station, you
will never live to see it completed!

A few seconds later the sign vanished and the screen went dark.

"Great Scott!" Mr. Swift exclaimed. "What happened to Kane?"

"He must have been overpowered by whoever sent that message!" Tom concluded. "We'd better contact the Key West police at once!"

Snatching up the phone, he asked Miss Trent to put through a call to Florida immediately. When the police captain came on the line, Tom gave him a quick report of what had happened and asked him to check on Kane's safety without a moment's delay.

Father and son waited tensely for nearly half an hour. Then the captain called back, but this time on the videophone.

"Your hunch was right," the police officer said as he appeared on the screen. "We found your telecaster slugged and unconscious. My men have given him first aid."

At that moment Kane stepped into view, a bandage on his head. His face was drawn and his movements were unsteady.

"Kane! Are you all right?" Tom demanded, alarmed by the man's appearance.

"Sure, I'm okay—aside from this goose egg on my

head," the telecaster replied with a sickly grin. "But I'd sure like to lay my hands on the guy who conked me!"

"Did you see him?"

Kane shook his head. "Sorry, skipper, but he took me completely by surprise. Must have sneaked in the door behind me while I was working at my desk."

"Don't worry about it," Mr. Swift spoke up. "And take things easy for a while, Kane."

The police captain promised to make every effort to find the criminal responsible for the attack, then Kane signed off.

"I'd like to hunt for him myself," Tom said heatedly.

As he and his father were discussing this latest move by their mysterious enemies, Bud phoned. He was thunderstruck when he heard what had happened to Kane and was all for going to Florida to take a hand.

"Not now," said Tom.

"What I called up for," said Bud, "was to see if you were ready yet to begin the search for the launching site of that missile that nearly finished us the day before yesterday."

"Yes, I am. Meet you at the heliplane hangar in five minutes!" Tom replied.

When he arrived there in a jeep, Bud was waiting with Harlan Ames and Phil Radnor. The ship had been rolled out of its hangar. The group climbed in and soon the whirring blades were lifting the heli-

A terrific blast rocked the hills

plane skyward. High aloft, Tom gunned the main jet, pressed a switch to retract the rotors, and sent the ship spearing forward through the blue.

En route to the spot where they expected to find the launching site, Tom told the security men about the attack on Kane. Radnor responded with a burst of anger, and Ames commented grimly, "So your unknown enemies are operating in Florida, too. Looks as if we're up against a bigger outfit than we realized."

"I'm afraid we are," Tom replied gravely. "Well, the first step is to find out who sent that missile and from where."

Assuming that the enemy missile had been launched in a straight-powered path, they figured the approximate location to be somewhere in the nearby Jasper range of hills which was intersected by winding streams.

To be on the safe side, Tom flew a wide reconnaissance over an area one mile square, centered on the spot which had been marked on the map. Yet a careful scrutiny of the terrain, even through powerful binoculars, yielded no clue to the launching site.

"Maybe they've camouflaged it," suggested Bud.

"Could be—if they haven't already moved everything out," agreed Tom. "Let's try a ground search."

After landing the heliplane, the group spread out to begin their hunt, but kept within shouting distance of one another.

Alone, Tom plodded along a shallow, rocky creek.

Suddenly his keen eyes detected a movement through a notch in the hills. Raising his binoculars, he felt a thrill of excitement. Framed in his field glasses was the hideous face of the Gorilla!

Yelling to his companions, Tom dashed forward. The others charged after him.

Beyond the hills, the creek widened into a good-sized pond, fringed with willows and brush. Without pausing, the group split up—Bud and Ames fanning out along one bank of the pond, with Radnor following Tom on the opposite side. Soon each pursuer had lost sight of his companions.

Tom felt sure that he was on the right track. This time, he was determined not to let the Gorilla get away!

"He's an enemy! There's no doubt about—"

At that moment a terrific blast rocked the hills. Tom was thrown violently to the ground by the force of the explosion!

CHAPTER 5

ZERO-G CHAMBER

AFTER THE EXPLOSION, Tom lay stunned for several moments. Dirt and debris rained down. Finally the atmosphere cleared and he staggered to his feet.

Were his friends all right, he wondered, or had they been injured by the blast? Running back toward the mouth of the pond, Tom was relieved to find Ames and Radnor unharmed. Their worried faces broke into smiles at sight of the young inventor.

A moment later Bud came hurrying up to join them. His T shirt was smudged with dirt, and blood trickled down one temple.

"Bud! Your forehead!" exclaimed Tom.

"Oh, I'm all right."

"What happened?"

Bud grimaced. "All of a sudden something went boom and it started raining rocks. One of 'em rained on me—that's all I know!"

Tom took a clean handkerchief from his pocket, moistened it in the creek, and washed Bud's wound. It proved to be only a slight cut.

Turning to the others, Tom said, "Let's find out where that explosion took place. Only this time we'd better watch our step."

The locale of the blast seemed to be just beyond high ground, near the far end of the pond. The rise was partly screened by trees, now shattered and stripped of their leaves by the explosion.

The four searchers advanced cautiously over the knoll. In the hollow beyond it, the blast had ripped a jagged hole in the ground. Trees and shrubs had been uprooted and buried under tons of dirt. Hardly a sprig of vegetation remained alive.

Alert for a possible ambush, Tom and his companions descended into the hollow. Several twisted steel girders and plates protruded from the debris.

Tom brushed away the dirt with his toe. "Looks as if this is where the missile came from, all right," he announced. "And here's what's left of the launching track."

"Do you think that explosion was an accident?" Bud asked.

Radnor shook his head. "More likely they blew up the place on purpose when the Gorilla saw us coming. He probably was acting as lookout."

Tom nodded grimly. "There's also the possibility that the blast was meant for us. Only it saved our necks by going off a bit too soon."

"Well, one thing we know for sure," commented Bud wryly. "Our enemies play for keeps!"

Before leaving the spot, Ames made an effort to pick up the trail of the Gorilla or anyone else who might have been stationed at the launching site. But the blast had wiped out any tracks or clues that might have guided him. Finally he gave up.

"Let's go!" he said.

When they arrived back at Swift Enterprises, Ames made a suggestion to Tom. "Why not make a sketch of this man you call the Gorilla? I'll have it photostated and sent to the police. We might turn up a lead on him."

"Good idea," Tom agreed. "I'll tackle it as soon as I get to my office. Come along."

The drawing was a sketchy but definite likeness of the mystery man, and Ames was sure that it would produce results. But a week later the security officer reported that their efforts had drawn a complete blank. Every branch of the police and FBI returned the same answer: *No information on this person in our files.*

"Maybe he's new at this crime business," remarked Bud. "Well, that'll make it even more difficult to trail him."

Tom, meanwhile, was busy night and day in the glass-walled laboratory building, working on plans for the enlarged space station. From time to time, his father would drop in to lend advice and encouragement.

On one such call, Mr. Swift found the young inventor slouched moodily at his workbench, staring at a paper covered with hastily scribbled calculations. "Having trouble, son?" he inquired sympathetically.

Tom nodded. "It's the air supply, Dad. I never realized until now the great amount of oxygen the crew of the space station will use up every day. The average man consumes about three pounds of air during a twenty-four-hour period. Even transporting oxygen in liquid form could mean a real supply problem."

"Perhaps it might be possible to *manufacture* your own oxygen," Mr. Swift suggested. "Or, at any rate, enough to supply part of your needs. Say, by a process of photosynthesis."

"You mean, by using green plants to give off oxygen?" Tom asked doubtfully.

"That's the idea. Of course no ordinary plants would do, but I seem to recall reading somewhere—"

The elder scientist's voice trailed off as he tugged thoughtfully at his lower lip. Suddenly he said, "I remember now! It was in the *Annual Review of Microbiology*. The writer mentioned some tiny one-celled water plants called chlorella—"

Tom snapped his fingers excitedly. "Of course! I read that, too. In strong sunshine they produce up to fifty times their own volume of oxygen per hour!"

"Correct!" Mr. Swift added. "And of course they would remove the carbon dioxide the men exhale. With a few tankfuls of such plants, I think you could supply the oxygen needs of your crew."

Tom revised his calculations in the light of this new oxygen supply. A moment later he looked up triumphantly.

"Dad, you're a wonder! I think chlorella may be the answer." Grinning, Tom added, "Why don't you come around here more often?"

"You seem to be doing all right by yourself," his father said, smiling. "By the way, what are you doing to offset the lack of gravity up in space? Have your station spin all the time to produce artificial gravity?"

Tom replied thoughtfully, "I'm not sure that's necessary, Dad. When Bud and I took our ride around the earth 1,075 miles up we were not bothered too much by the feeling of weightlessness that comes with lack of the earth's gravity holding you down."

"But you were aloft only a little over two hours," Mr. Swift replied. "Some experts believe that human beings could not survive long without gravity. Their nervous systems might not be able to stand it for extended periods of time."

"Only an experiment will prove it," Tom said. "I have a hunch that a selected crew *could* learn to live and work in a weightless state for longer than we think. And what's more, Dad, I intend to find out!"

"How?"

Tom went on to say that a feeling of weightlessness was not unlike a feeling of helplessness.

"One would have to learn how to do everything a different way—eat, drink, move, work. And I see no reason why some of that can't be done right here."

"You're way ahead of me, Tom," his father admitted. "Have you cracked the impossible, son? Are you going to produce zero gravity here on earth?"

"No, Dad. But I am going to build a transparent, sealed room outdoors about twenty feet square and fifteen feet high, which we'll call the Zero-G chamber."

"Yes. And then?"

Tom considered for a moment, drumming his fingers on the workbench. "Well, you know how a piece of metal can be floated between the poles of a rapidly pulsating magnetic field. I'll use the same principle."

"But human beings aren't made of metal."

"No, but I believe a metal suit could be designed to produce the same effect. A person floating in the air chamber would feel mighty helpless. Now if he had to find out how fast or slow he had to propel himself to try to reach, say, a hammer that was floating too, and then go after nails and wood also in the air—"

"I see," said Mr. Swift. "You'd be overcoming some of the problems you'd meet up in space."

"Exactly. I'd add this test to the others that my crew would have to pass in order to become spacemen."

The elder inventor looked impressed. "You may have something there, son. It's certainly a good idea. And if it's found that continuous lack of gravity isn't advisable in your space station, you can always start it spinning to set up artificial gravity."

"Right."

As the work-filled days went by there were other visitors to Tom's lab. Arv Hanson came to talk over ideas and show Tom a model of the revised space station. Hank Sterling made numerous trips to discuss the foundry patterns needed for casting metal parts to be used in the project.

One day Tom looked up from his work and smiled. He had just heard the sound of a booming voice and high-heeled cowboy boots.

"Well, brand my three-toed bronc, what kind o' doo-funny you workin' on now, Tom?"

The speaker was Chow Winkler, a bowlegged, weather-beaten, roly-poly former range cook from Texas. Now the head chef for all Swift expeditions, he had been vacationing since the last trip.

"Hi, Chow!" Tom grinned. The sight of the lovable, good-natured Westerner always cheered him up when he was troubled by tough, scientific problems. "I just got a brilliant idea!"

"Let's hear it."

"We'll take out a patent on that shirt you're wearing and put it on the market as a sure cure for color blindness!"

Chow chuckled as he looked down at his loud red-yellow-and-purple Western-style shirt. Far from taking offense, he was proud of his spectacular shirt collection.

"You jest say the word, Tom, an' I'll wire San Antone this minute for a tailor-made duplicate in your size! But what in tarnation is this?" he added, picking up one of Arv Hanson's models from Tom's workbench. "Don't tell me you're goin' in for designin' chuck-wagon wheels?"

"Chuck-wagon wheels?" Tom laughed. "Listen, Chow, that's a model of the space station I'm working on."

The cook squinted suspiciously, then shoved back his ten-gallon hat and scratched his balding head.

"You pullin' my leg, Tom?" he inquired.

"No, on the level, Chow," Tom replied. "This is really what our space station will look like if we ever get it built. You see, each spoke of the wheel will actually be part of a rocket. But we won't connect them to the hub until after we shoot them out into space."

"You mean, people are goin' to live inside this contraption?"

"That's right. The whole thing will be hollow. And each spoke will be a separate compartment for one particular use."

"Like for instance?" Chow queried.

"Well, some will be observatories, others labs. Some will be for manufacturing our new solar batteries, and some will be used for broadcasting or telecasting. Of course the crew will be able to go from one compartment to another, either through the hub or through these connecting alleyways that form the outer rim of the wheel."

"And how would a critter go about gettin' inside in the first place?"

"Through one of these ports at the outer end of each spoke," Tom said, pointing to the model. "Whenever a supply rocket comes up from earth, it will nose right into an opening and unload."

Chow scratched his chin and scowled thoughtfully. "I still don't savvy why the blamed thing is shaped like a wheel. You figger on havin' it turn around up there in the sky?"

"We *could* make it rotate, Chow," replied Tom, "if we wanted to set up artificial gravity."

"How's that again?"

Tom attempted to explain. "You see, Chow, once we get out there in space, everything will seem weightless. We'll just float around with nowhere to fall to, because there won't *be* any up or down. But some people might not find that very pleasant. So the answer would be to start the wheel turning."

"What good would that do?" Chow asked, still mystified.

"Ever seen what happens if you twirl a ball around and around on the end of a string?"

"Why, brand my radarscope, any jughead knows that. The speed keeps the string taut with the ball bein' pushed out."

"Right. So if the *wheel* started spinning around, everything inside would tend to push out toward the rim. In other words, for the spacemen inside each spoke, 'up' would mean toward the wheel hub and 'down' would mean toward the rim."

Chow mulled this over silently for a while, then began muttering to himself as he tried to figure out Tom's explanation. Finally he burst out in despair:

"Sufferin' coyotes, Tom! Down is out, an' up is in, an'— I jest don't get the hang o' that nohow. If cookin' grub on a space station is goin' to mess a feller all up that-a-way, I'd rather stay put right here on the ground!"

Tom shook with laughter but added consolingly, "Don't worry, Chow. I don't believe our station will have to do any turning, anyhow." But the veteran cowpoke merely clumped off, shaking his head glumly.

Tom was in for a surprise, however, for early the next morning Chow showed up at the laboratory and announced that he had changed his mind.

"You mean you want to come with us when we set up our space station?" Tom asked.

"Yep. If you go, I go. Ain't no one goin' to say old Chow is scared to take a chance."

"That's the spirit," Tom said. "But first you'll have to pass some tests."

"You jest lead the way, Tom. I reckon that there sky wheel o' yours can't be much worse'n some o' the buckin' broncs I've tangled with in my time!"

"Okay, Chow—if you really want to try." Tom got up from his drawing board. "Come on. I'll have Bud start you off on the tests."

A short time later Chow found himself strapped in the gondola of a huge centrifuge. "This is to find out how well you can stand rocket acceleration," Bud told him.

After checking and adjusting the controls, Bud pressed the starting switch. Slowly at first, then with ever-increasing speed, the long, tubular-steel arm supporting the gondola began spinning round and round.

Inside the device, Chow felt as though a giant hand were squashing him down into the seat with crushing force. His face muscles sagged like the jowls of a bulldog. Breathing became harder and harder. Just when it seemed as if he could stand it no more, the feeling of weight began to leave him and the gondola slowed down.

Bud opened the door and unstrapped him. Chow climbed out, somewhat wobbly, but otherwise in good shape.

"Well, how do you feel, old-timer?" Bud asked a bit anxiously.

"Fit as a fiddle an' rarin' to go!" Chow boasted. "But that ain't sayin' I could do much cookin' in one o' them gallopin' chuck wagons. Might work out better all around if I cooked all the grub right here on the ground 'fore we ever took off." And he added with a chuckle, "Reckon I'll have to learn to make gravity biscuits!"

"You won't have to—your regular biscuits are heavy enough as it is!" But when Bud saw the hurt look in the cook's eyes, he hastened to reassure Chow that he was only joking.

The second test was scheduled for the following day. This time, Chow was placed in the altitude chamber to determine his reaction under low pressure. Bud showed him how to adjust his oxygen mask, then closed the hatch.

Turning on the air pump and opening a valve, Bud began to exhaust the air from the chamber. As the needle on the pressure gauge flickered downward, Bud watched Chow's reaction through the glass observation window.

For a time, everything seemed to be going well. Then, suddenly, Chow slumped forward—limp and unconscious!

CHAPTER 6

VACATION BOUND

STARING through the small window, Bud felt maddeningly helpless. What could have happened to Chow? Perhaps he was seriously ill! Bud wondered anxiously if he had decompressed the old cowpoke too fast and thus brought on an attack of the dreaded "bends."

Finally the pressure needle pointed back to normal and Bud ripped open the hatch. He scooped up the limp figure in his arms and carried Chow out of the chamber.

Placing the Texan on a bench, Bud quickly unstrapped his oxygen mask. He noticed that Chow was breathing in loud, deep gasps.

Bud stared at the cook sharply. For the first time, an odd suspicion occurred to him. Nevertheless, he loosened Chow's shirt collar and began patting his cheeks and rubbing his wrists.

As he did, Chow's breathing became louder and deeper than ever. Then his head lolled over to one side and his lower jaw dropped open. A moment later Bud's suspicion became a certainty. Chow was snoring!

Bud stopped short as if he had been stung by a wasp. He shook his patient roughly. "Chow! Wake up!"

The cook's eyes flickered open. He mumbled a sleepy reply. Then he caught sight of Bud and sat up, blinking in surprise. "Sa-a-ay, what in thunderation's goin' on here?" he demanded.

"You just fell asleep in the altitude chamber, that's what!" snapped Bud irritably. "Had me scared half out of my wits thinking something was wrong!"

"Asleep?" Chow echoed, then grinned sheepishly. "Brand my space suit, I shouldn't 'a' stayed up to look at that Western on TV last night! I ain't fit for nuthin' the next day after I been up watchin' a late movie."

Chow was so apologetic that Bud burst out laughing. "All right, put your mask on and get back inside. But no more doping off in there, or you flunk this test for sure!"

This time, Chow came through with flying colors, and promised to report wide awake for future tests.

Later that morning Bud dropped into Tom's private laboratory, where the young inventor got a hearty chuckle out of Chow's experience. Tom showed his friend the newly completed plans for the Zero-G chamber, in which he hoped to learn how to work while floating in air.

"Sounds like a fourth-dimensional fun house at a Martian carnival," Bud remarked. "But if you say it works, I'll buy it."

Tom laughed. Then he said seriously, "Bud, I'm placing you in charge of all applicants for our space station expedition. Put them through the same routine you're giving Chow, and if they pass, we'll end up with the Zero-G chamber test after I've made it myself. If possible, I'd prefer men from Enterprises who are already cleared for security."

"Righto, skipper!" Bud promised. "I'll pick you out the hottest crew of space jockeys this side of Venus!"

But ten days later Bud showed up at Tom's lab wearing a long face. "Bad news," he reported. "So far, I've been able to find only three men who are fit to work at the space station." He explained that not so many had applied for the expedition as he had expected. Of these, only the three mentioned had been able to pass the rigorous tests for space flight.

Tom frowned thoughtfully. "Looks as though we'll have to go outside our own outfit," he remarked. He suggested several men from the Swift Construction Company plant and Bud promised to check them.

When Tom arrived home that night, he slumped down in an easy chair, completely fagged out. Later he ate little at dinner. His mother and Sandy knew the signs of too much concentrated work.

"Don't you think you're overdoing a bit, dear?" Mrs. Swift suggested gently. "If only you'd take a short vacation, I'm sure you'd feel much better—and get on with your work faster, too."

"I'd like to, Mother, but I just can't break away," he said.

"But, Tom," Sandy spoke up, "a vacation needn't mean twiddling your thumbs or wasting time!" She crossed the room to drop on a hassock beside his chair. "You could use your vacation to help your space station project."

"Just how would I do that?" her brother inquired, smiling doubtfully.

"By flying to Florida and looking for a clue to the person who knocked out Kane. The police haven't found him yet. We could make it a foursome—you and Bud and Phyl and I!"

"That's a very good idea," Mrs. Swift approved. "You could stay with the Lawsons. I had a letter from them last month, inviting you young folks down for a visit."

"Oh, Tom, please say yes!" Sandy urged. "We could have so much fun."

The Lawsons, a retired elderly couple, were long-time friends of the Swift family. They now lived in a large waterfront house at Key West.

Tom was greatly tempted by Sandy's suggestion about combining work and play—by the thought of tracking down Kane's attacker and having frequent dips in the warm blue waters around the Florida Keys. Finally he let himself be persuaded.

Bud and Phyl also were enthusiastic about the idea. Two days later the foursome took off in the heliplane.

Winging their way out of Shopton, they sighted another of the experimental balloons belonging to the Quik Battery Corporation. Tom was laughingly giving it a wide berth when his sister cried out, "Look! It happened again!" All eyes turned to see the balloon disintegrate in shreds and the tiny parachute start earthward with its cargo of instruments.

"Oh, brother!" Bud exclaimed. "Let's hope we were out of range of that aerial camera, Tom, or you may get slapped with another lawsuit!"

With the heliplane speeding through the skies under jet power, it was not long before the travelers were flying over Georgia. Seated beside Tom at the controls, Phyl asked him how he hoped to pick up the trail of the person who had attacked Kane and sent the mysterious warning.

"Chances are the gang knows what we're up to," Tom replied. "I have a hunch that they'll come tagging after us soon enough, without our even bothering to look for them."

Presently Sandy begged for a chance to handle the heliplane and Tom willingly turned over the controls. He had the utmost confidence in her flying skill. The pretty blond girl had proved an apt pupil of her father and brother in handling all types of aircraft.

"You may find it a bit tricky at first, converting back and forth from jet to rotors," Tom explained. "But you'll soon get the feel of it."

Besides demonstrating the main operating controls, Tom also showed his sister how the wing tips were hinged to fold downward at the press of a button, so the wing tanks could serve as pontoons, for landing or taxiing on water. She came down twice in convenient spots to try it out, once on land, once on a deserted river. In a short time Sandy was flying the remarkable craft like a veteran.

"Oh, Tom, this ship handles like a dream!" she exclaimed, as they neared Key West.

Soon they were above the long white ribbon of highway connecting the small islets that dot the sparkling blue waters of the straits. Smoothly, Sandy brought the heliplane down on the water.

The Lawsons were there to meet them and drove the young people to their home. After lunch their hostess smilingly said, "I know you'll want to be on the beach as much as possible, so go right out there. The water is perfect today."

It was not long before Tom and the others were sprawled in swim suits on the dazzling white sands of the beach, under the shade of a huge striped umbrella. Other vacationers lolled nearby.

Though conversation was light for a time, it finally turned to the space station. "Have you de-

cided where your rockets for it will be launched?"
Phyl asked Tom.

"Dad's negotiating for a site on a Pacific island
near the equator," Tom replied. "The launching
area has to be somewhere in mid-ocean, so that the
first two stages of each rocket can be dropped off
safely after they're burned out."

Sketching in the sand with a sea shell, Tom went
on to describe how the rockets would take off straight
upward, then gradually tilt to an easterly course.
After climbing to a height of 22,300 miles, they
would finally level off.

"After that they will travel in one orbit, keeping
opposite the same spot on earth at all times."

"You mean the space station will stay in that location?" Phyl asked.

"Yes."

"Good night!" said Sandy. "Won't it have to travel
horribly fast to do that?"

"A little over 6,800 miles per hour." Tom
grinned. "Which works out to about 1.9 miles per
second."

Phyl shivered. "Golly, it makes me dizzy just to
think of it!"

Chuckling, Tom added, "All of us are whirling
through space pretty fast right now. In fact, a person
at the equator is traveling at a speed of almost a
thousand miles per hour. We're doing a little less."

"No wonder I feel so lightheaded," said Bud.

"And all this time I thought it was just the thrill of two beautiful girls."

"Stop spoiling his illusions, Tom!" joked Sandy.

"Seriously," Bud went on, "what about the heat from all the solar radiation out there in space? Won't that run pretty high too?"

"You're so right," Tom admitted ruefully. "I figure that the outside temperature of the space station may run close to 1,500 degrees Fahrenheit. Which means we'll need a terrific cooling system for the setup."

"And a heating system, too," Sandy put in, recalling a discussion with her father. "Dad says it gets down to 459 degrees below zero during the two hours of darkness."

"Really?" Phyl was surprised. "The earth doesn't get that cold."

Tom explained that the earth and its air blanket retained the sun's heat during the night hours. "It might seem chilly," he added, "but by comparison with outer space, a zero winter's night is mighty cozy."

"What's being done to lick this heat problem?" Bud asked.

"Well, for one thing," Tom said, "the station will be built of magnesium with a highly polished, almost white surface. In that way, it will reflect the heat rays rather than absorb them. Also, the station will be coated with Tomasite for further protection.

And inside, it will have a double wall of thin steel with more insulation sandwiched in between."

"Okay, you can stop right there." Sandy laughed, scrambling to her feet. "This is supposed to be a vacation, too, so let's forget all that space chatter for a while and go for a swim. Last one in is a big nothing!"

Shouting and laughing, the four young people raced across the sand and plunged into the rolling blue-green surf. A moment later they were cavorting like dolphins.

When they emerged, dripping and refreshed, they strolled back to the spot where they had erected their beach umbrella. Beneath it, someone had stuck a pop bottle upright in the sand. Phyl was the first to notice it and gave a cry of surprise. In the mouth of the bottle was a rolled-up piece of paper.

"The Lawsons must have left this," said Tom as he plucked out the paper and unrolled it. But the message was not from their friends. The printed words read:

> TOM SWIFT:
> LAY OFF YOUR DETECTING AND STAY
> HOME. THIS IS YOUR LAST WARNING!

CHAPTER 7

QUEER FOOTPRINTS

AS TOM READ the threatening note, Sandy clutched his arm fearfully. "Oh, Tom," she murmured, "I shouldn't have talked you into coming down here after all! Maybe we should fly back to Shopton at once."

"And let those phonies scare us out of our vacation? Not on your life, Sis!" Tom patted Sandy's hand reassuringly. "Just relax and let's see if we can figure this thing out."

"Don't you think you should take the warning seriously?" Phyl asked in a worried voice.

"Sure, but that's no reason for panic. One thing is certain—an enemy is within reach and may be still on the beach. If we could only lay our hands on him!"

"Which may not be so easy," commented Bud, looking around.

The others, too, scanned the area which was

dotted with people. Some were stretched out on the sand, sun-bathing, with their eyes protected by dark glasses. Others were chatting or playing cards under beach umbrellas. Tom questioned several persons. None had noticed anyone suspicious.

"It's hopeless!" Sandy groaned. "How can you possibly identify the person who planted that note in the bottle?"

Frowning, Tom studied the maze of footprints in the sand all around their umbrella. "It doesn't look as though these tracks will do us much good, either."

"Wait a minute!" Bud exclaimed. "I'm not so sure!"

At the note of excitement in his friend's voice Tom looked up. "Find something?" he asked.

"Could be." Bud pointed at the sand. "Seems to me I can make out one particular set of prints leading away from the pop bottle. You folks stay here. Let me see if I can follow them."

Tom and the girls watched anxiously as Bud trudged away, stepping carefully so as not to obliterate the prints and keeping his eyes focused on the sand. He headed toward a cement walk, thronged with strollers in colorful beach costumes.

After reaching the walk, Bud paused for a moment, looking up and down. Then he turned around and plodded back slowly. His face registered disappointment.

"No good," he reported glumly when he came within earshot. "Whoever the guy was, he played it smart and left via the walk. He knew that we couldn't follow his tracks on a concrete pavement!"

"What about the prints themselves?" Sandy asked. "Any identifying marks?"

"I didn't notice any," Bud replied.

"Let's take a closer look," Tom suggested.

Most of the footprints were little more than vague blurs. But one set of prints was fairly sharp. Tom and the others crouched down to examine them.

At first glance the prints seemed perfectly ordinary. Then Sandy exclaimed, "Look! Isn't this toe mark shorter than it should be?"

She pointed to the print of the great toe on the left foot. It was shorter than the second toe just beside it, and also markedly shorter than its mate on the right foot.

"Good for you, Sandy!" Tom said.

"But I still don't see how it's going to help us," Bud muttered.

Phyl smiled and said, "Why not? All you have to do is go around like the prince's messenger in the Cinderella story and ask every man you meet to take off his shoes!"

The others burst out laughing, and for the time being the search was postponed. None of the young people forgot the incident, however.

During the next two days, Tom's mysterious enemies made no further moves and the searchers got no additional clues. Not even one bather with a short great toe appeared on the beach.

Tom enjoyed his vacation and spent most of the time loafing in the sun. Yet his inventive mind was never inactive. One day he seemed to be dozing on the sand when the others saw him suddenly snap his fingers.

"What gives?" Bud asked, looking up from a quiz game he was playing with the girls.

Tom raised himself on one elbow, an excited glint in his eye. "I think I may have the answer to what's wrong with my solar battery!" he exclaimed. "I'll use a brand-new alloy that just occurred to me!"

"Hot rockets!" Bud grinned. "Don't you ever stop inventing?"

Tom ignored the gibe. "I'll make some as soon as we get back, and send it up in a rocket for a test. If it works, I'll name it sol-alloy. Don't you think we've had enough—?"

"No, we haven't had enough vacation," Sandy interrupted. "And besides, we haven't found the man who sent you the threatening messages."

Early the next morning, she and Phyl went down to the beach for a dip. The two girls were tossing a beach ball back and forth, before going into the water, when suddenly Phyl stopped the game. She came close to Sandy and whispered excitedly:

"Look at that man over there—the one with the striped bathing trunks! And notice his left foot. It has a short great toe to match that queer print we saw in the sand."

Sandy stole a glance in the direction Phyl had indicated. The man lay stretched out on the sand with a rolled-up towel across his eyes to protect them from the sun.

The girls looked at each other knowingly and studied him for a moment. His black hair was close-cropped, and though his face was partly hidden by the towel, they judged him to be about thirty years old. Sandy turned to Phyl and hurriedly whispered a plan for finding out more about him.

Casually the girls moved their umbrella close to the spot where the man was lying, then resumed their game of beach ball. Sandy purposely let the ball go past her. It landed several yards away and rolled on to bump up against the man's legs. He woke up with a start.

Sandy hurried to recover the ball and apologized profusely. "Oh, I'm terribly sorry!" she said.

The man regarded her with a friendly grin. It went through her mind that he certainly did not look like a criminal. He was, no doubt, one of the suave variety Sandy decided.

"Don't bother to apologize," the stranger said pleasantly.

Sandy cocked her head and assumed a puzzled frown. "Aren't you the man who lives next door to the Lawsons?" she inquired.

"I'm afraid not." He laughed. "But if that would make us neighbors, I wish I were."

He *was* smooth! Sandy laughed. She and Phyl abandoned their game and reclined under the beach umbrella. The conversation with the suspect was resumed.

The stranger told them that he was an ex-Army officer, recently separated from the Signal Corps. He had come to Florida for some sunshine and a much-needed rest.

"By the way," he added, "may I introduce myself? My name is Kenneth Horton."

"I'm Sandra Swift," responded Sandy, "and this is my friend, Phyllis Newton."

Having learned what they wished to know, the girls presently broke off the conversation and went for a swim.

"Are you sure it was wise to tell him our names?" inquired Phyl with a worried frown.

"What's the difference?" Sandy replied. "If he's one of the men who have been spying on Tom, he already knows who we are. If not, well—"

"Let's hurry back and tell the boys what we found out!" Phyl urged.

Returning to the Lawsons', the girls gave a full account of their meeting to Tom and Bud. The boys promptly raced toward the beach for a look at Horton.

"So he's the one who slipped you that warning!" Bud cried, doubling his fists. "Well, let's find out how big he talks, face to face!"

But Tom held his friend by the arm. "Take it easy, pal. We'll notify the FBI and let them deal with him. We'd need their help, anyhow, to check on his Army background."

After contacting the government agency, Tom made plans to leave.

"We've accomplished a lot here, thanks to you girls," he said. "But I really must get back to the lab."

The next morning the young people took off and landed at Shopton just before noon. Immediately after lunch Tom plunged into work in his metallurgical laboratory to try out the new alloy he had thought of for his solar battery.

Bud watched with intense curiosity as his friend smelted small quantities of several metals together in a small electric furnace. He tested the result. Not satisfied, Tom repeated the process over and over, using different proportions of the ingredients. Finally he felt he had the right combination. The alloy had a high degree of malleability.

"Now we'll put this through the rollers," he told Bud, leading the way to a workshop full of heavy equipment.

Tom pushed a wall button, setting a series of highly polished steel rollers into action. Into them he fed the hot metal, which finally was reduced to a thin sheet.

"Your mother couldn't have done better with a rolling pin," Bud quipped, as Tom trimmed and cut the foil in a shearing machine. "So this is sol-alloy," he remarked, picking up one of the sheets to examine it.

"Let's call it sol-alloy, Type One," replied Tom with a rueful grin. "We may have to work all the way down to Type Sixteen before I find exactly what I want."

"What happens now?" asked Bud.

"I'll send this stuff up in a rocket from Fearing Island to be irradiated," Tom replied. "Then we'll use it in a battery cell and test it."

"Sounds good," said Bud. "But don't ask me to go up with it! I might blow up with this sol-alloy stuff."

"Could be," said Tom. "I'll send up another dummy." The young inventor grinned as he affectionately slapped his pal on the back.

Fearing Island was the rocket proving grounds of Swift Enterprises. It was a thumb-shaped stretch of sand dunes and scrubgrass, located off the Atlantic Coast—a government restricted area, guarded by an elaborate security setup. This included a double ring of robot drone planes, which constantly circled above the island.

After radioing ahead that they were coming, the boys took off in the heliplane, accompanied by Hank Sterling. When they were in sight of the island, Tom identified himself to the control tower. The dispatcher flipped a switch to neutralize the drones, and the sleek helicopter jet craft hovered in to land on the island's airfield.

"What kind of rocket are you going to use to test the sol-alloy?" Hank asked.

"A small projectile," Tom answered. "I'm having a special porthole machined in the nose."

He, Bud, and Hank went at once to see it, carrying the foil with them.

In the nose of the rocket, over the porthole, was a quartz faceplate which opened and closed automatically. The sol-alloy sheet was mounted beneath it. When closed, the plate would protect the foil from heat and oxygen during the flight up and down through the atmosphere. Once beyond the atmosphere, the window would swing open to permit the sol-alloy to receive the maximum amount of solar radiation.

Take-off was scheduled for noon the next day, to ensure the strongest possible rays from the sun. Fifteen minutes beforehand, Tom inserted the flight tape in the automatic pilot. This would guide the rocket back to a safe landing on the island. Finally, the rocket was sealed.

A short time later the boys stood at the rail of the high tracking platform. Hank's voice echoed over the public-address system:

"All personnel leave the launching area at once! X minus two minutes!"

Tom counted off the seconds on his wrist watch. Then a thunderous explosion rocked the ground. Belching flames, the rocket rose from its launching tower and zoomed away.

Inside the tracking room, a radar crew was already plotting its course. As the rocket disappeared into the blue, Tom and Bud raced inside to watch also. Tense moments went by.

Presently Tom said, "She's reached maximum height now—450 miles. If the porthole is open—"

"The old sol-alloy is really getting a sun bath," Bud finished.

"The rocket's starting back," Hank announced.

"Bud! Hit the ground

A few minutes later a resounding *boom* sounded from the sky, followed by the appearance of a white vapor trail.

"Thar she blows!" Bud shouted, elated by the sound of the rocket as it penetrated the denser atmosphere.

They watched the vapor trail of supercooled-water droplets lengthen as the rocket arrowed in for a landing. The boys raced toward the beach to observe the results of the irradiated sol-alloy.

Nearing the rocket, Tom was stunned to see a glow through the porthole. Instantly he dropped to the earth, yelling:

"Bud! Hit the ground and cover your eyes!"

and cover your eyes!"

CHAPTER 8

PERIL FROM THE SEA

BUD FLUNG HIMSELF headlong in the sand after Tom. Both boys shielded their eyes with their arms. A split second later came a blinding flash of light from the rocket!

Even with their eyelids squeezed shut, they saw the dazzling brilliance of the glare. As the light faded away, Tom opened his eyes cautiously and saw Bud scrambling to his feet.

"What in the name of aerodynamics was that?" he gasped.

Tom grinned wryly and said, "Crazy as it may sound, that flash of light proved our experiment is a big success."

"How so?"

"Come here. I'll show you." Tom led the way to the burned-out rocket and pointed to the now-blackened porthole. "Notice what's happened to the metal frame around the quartz window?" he re-marked.

"Wow!" Bud exclaimed. "It's fused solid to the metal shell of the rocket. The heat from that flash must have been terrific."

"Right," Tom agreed. "Which means our battery picked up a sizable charge out there in space."

"Then this foil you developed is going to work!" Bud responded enthusiastically.

"Well, the sol-alloy *did* become energized by the solar radiation," Tom explained. "In other words, a big percentage of its free electrons was energized to highly excited states and trapped there on the surface of the metal foil. But the trouble is they didn't *stay* trapped."

"You mean the battery short-circuited somehow?"

Tom nodded. "That's what caused the flash. Apparently the sol-alloy is very unstable when it's in a charged state. So now the problem is to figure out a desensitizer for the stuff—something to keep it from discharging all of a sudden as it did just now."

By this time, Hank Sterling and the other engineers had arrived on the scene. They gathered around the boys, listening to Tom's explanation.

"What happens now?" Hank asked the young inventor. "Do you want this rocket taken back to the lab for examination?"

"Right," said Tom. "Looks as if we'll have to use a torch on it."

The rocket was hoisted on a carriage and hauled

to the laboratory building. Tom and Bud stood by, watching through goggles, as a welder used an acetylene torch to cut apart the fused sections. Then Tom removed the sol-alloy from the battery inside the rocket and held it up to the light. The once-shiny metal foil was covered with a dull-gray coating.

"It oxidized completely when that flash occurred," Tom muttered.

"Cheer up, pal," Bud said, clapping him on the back. "Just be glad you didn't oxidize along with it."

Tom smiled, then became serious. "If a commercial battery ever failed that way," he said, "no buyer would touch another with a ten-foot pole. It could ruin our whole market overnight."

During the next few days, Tom used the island's facilities to work on a desensitizer.

One morning his father telephoned from the mainland. "How's the work coming, son?"

Tom told him and said, "I will be ready for another battery test early next week."

"Fine! I called to let you know that I'm taking off for the Pacific this evening."

"To see about our new launching site for the space station?"

"Yes. It's a tiny spot called Loonaui—hardly a speck on the map. We've just received clearance."

"That's great, Dad!" Tom exclaimed. "By the time you get back, I'll have all the kinks ironed out of the solar battery. Have a good trip!"

Tom hung up and plunged back into his work,

more enthusiastic than ever. He was thrilled by the exciting prospect ahead.

With luck, he would lead the first expedition into outer space and establish a new earth satellite!

As the week end approached, the young inventor struggled over his problem. But at last he felt that he had it licked. Late Saturday night, Bud came to watch him complete the assembly of a battery to be used in the new test.

"Hey, what happened to the color of your sol-alloy?" he asked with a puzzled look. "It's darker than it was."

"That's because of the desensitizer I've mixed with it, so that the stuff won't pop off like a flash bulb the second it gets down to our atmosphere," Tom replied.

The young inventor explained that he had used as a desensitizing agent a trace amount of a transition metal sulfide. He had incorporated it in the sol-alloy when it was smelted. "And now we'll put together a four-cell battery," he said.

"What happens if the old sol-alloy oxidizes again?" Bud asked.

"It'll blow the rocket to smithereens, Bud. But I don't think that will happen this time."

Tom rolled up four sheets of the sol-alloy and inserted them into cylindrical cells made of a plastic he had invented which he called catalium. Then he filled the cells with liquid ammonia under pressure. As each cell was filled, Tom sealed it off. Finally, when all the cells were ready, he assembled them in a battery case made of catalium. He handed it to Bud who gave a surprised whistle.

"This is so light a child could lift it easily. Man, wait until the automobile makers get wind of this!"

Tom chuckled. "Bud, if that one battery you're holding works out, it'll supply enough power to run a whole fleet of cars!"

At noon Monday, Tom and Bud eagerly watched from the tracking platform as the second experimental rocket took off, carrying the new battery.

Tom glanced at his wrist watch. "Well, here's hoping," he muttered to Bud. "If this test—"

He was interrupted by a voice shouting his name. "Tom! Come in here quick!"

The boys whirled around to see George Dilling beckoning to them from the control room, an excited look on his face. Dilling was the chief radioman on Fearing Island, and was in charge of the radar-tracking crew at the moment.

"What's up, George? Anything wrong?" Tom demanded as he and Bud made a dash to investigate.

"Nothing to do with the rocket. It's the oscilloscope! A message is coming through from your space friends."

Dilling referred to the mysterious beings from another planet who had been communicating with the Swifts by mathematical symbols. The first message had arrived on a strange meteorlike missile which had landed on the grounds of Swift Enterprises.

Since then, several communications had been received and decoded by Tom and his father. Mr. Swift had kept a record of all the symbols and had compiled a dictionary. The messages indicated that the senders were intelligent beings who had mastered the problems of space travel—except one. They wished to visit the earth but were unable to penetrate our atmosphere.

When Tom and Bud reached the oscilloscope, they saw a series of weird symbols appearing. One of the engineers had already copied several of them on a sheet of paper, which he now shoved at Tom.

"Howlin' headwinds!" Bud cried out. "That machine's going crazy!"

The impulses were coming through stronger and faster than ever before. Tom jotted down the symbols at top speed. Many of them he recognized at a glance from previous messages.

Suddenly an odd symbol which Tom had never seen began to take shape on the scope. But before he could copy it, the machine went dead!

Tom groaned as he checked the instrument hastily. "The pulses were coming through with so much power that they burned out the cathode-ray tube!" he said, disappointed.

"What does the message say?" Bud asked impatiently.

"Give me time," replied the young inventor. "I haven't Dad's space dictionary here, so it may take awhile to translate this."

Just then, one of the radar trackers announced that the rocket they had sent up was now arcing downward. Tom shoved pencil and paper into a pocket and ran outside.

"Come on, Bud!" he called. "Let's get to the beach and find out how the battery worked this time. We can translate the message later!"

Together, the boys sprinted down the metal stairway of the tracking platform. They arrived breathless at the waterfront, where a number of crewmen were already standing by.

"Here she comes!" warned Hank Sterling, waving back several of the men.

The sleek steel-gray missile hurtled down from the sky, leveled off over the choppy waters, and streaked for the island. With a *whoosh,* it slowed to a gliding stop on the sand.

"Bud, look! There's no glow from the porthole!" Tom shouted triumphantly.

Before he could dash toward the rocket, Hank grabbed his arm and pointed out to sea with a cry of alarm. Beyond the outer ring of drone planes, a tremendous geyser of water spouted high into the air!

The other crewmen saw it, too—and something else as well. A shout went up, "Tidal wave!"

A wall of water ten feet high seemed to have arisen from nowhere. It bore down on the island with tremendous speed.

The men stared, hypnotized, awaking to their

danger only when Tom cried out, "Run for your lives!".

With one accord, they dashed for higher ground. But they had waited too long. With a loud roar, the wave rolled over the beach and engulfed them.

Tom and his friends were sucked under help-lessly!

CHAPTER 9

A DARING RESCUE

LASHING WAVES surged over Tom's head. His eyes were blinded by the pounding salt spray, his nose and mouth choked with water. Again and again he fought his way above the surface, gasping for air. But each time a fresh wall of brine thundered over him.

Frantic, Tom felt the current sweeping him toward the deep and treacherous offshore channel! Once he caught a fleeting glimpse of his friends struggling nearby. It was every man for himself!

His lungs aching, Tom finally righted himself and struck out for the shore line. Pounded and battered, he at last reached land. He stumbled a few paces up the beach, then sprawled headlong in the wet sand.

It was several moments before Tom could get his breath. As he sat up, a hand clutched his shoulder.

"Bud!" Tom exclaimed, turning around. "Thank heavens you're safe!"

"But slightly waterlogged," his friend said, wringing out his jersey. "How about you?"

"I feel as if I'd swallowed a couple of gallons of ocean."

Tom got to his feet a bit unsteadily. A few yards away he saw Hank Sterling lending a hand to a crewman emerging from the surf. Other members of the rocket station were scattered along the beach in various stages of recovery.

"Are we all here?" asked Tom, trudging over to Hank. Bud followed at his heels.

"I'd better check and make sure," replied the engineer.

The water had calmed down, and Tom could see a rescue boat some distance away, speeding around the point. Evidently it had been summoned from the north dock by an alarm from the control tower.

"Will Barrow is missing!" Hank cried out. "Has anyone seen him?"

Others came hurrying up, shocked by the news. Barrow, a skilled technician, was elderly and somewhat frail. Had he succumbed in the pounding surf?

"There he is!" All heads turned as Bud pointed out across the water. Far from shore, they saw a man's head bob and disappear among the waves.

Tom's face paled. He thought of Barrow's wife and family—and of having to tell them that Will had perished while working on one of the Swift projects.

"I'm going after him," he announced, kicking off his shoes.

"Don't be crazy, Tom!" exclaimed Hank, grabbing his arm. "You're in no condition for a swim like that! The rescue boat will pick him up!"

"It won't get there in time!" Tom gritted his teeth. "Will doesn't stand a chance!"

Jerking free from the arms that sought to restrain him, the young inventor plunged into the water. Swimming with fast, powerful strokes, he headed toward the drowning man.

In Tom's exhausted state, this fresh struggle with the sea was almost too much to endure. His breath was coming in painful gasps, and his arms ached. But he kept battling his way forward with one thought in mind.

The next thing Tom knew, he and Will

He had to save Will Barrow!

Moments seemed like hours before Will's head and shoulders loomed into view. He was struggling weakly in the swirling gray-green waters.

Summoning all his strength, Tom knifed forward and reached the man's side. With one arm he encircled Will's chest. With the other he struck out for the shore line, which seemed miles away. Before he had gone a dozen yards, Tom knew he could never make it. He felt dizzy and his heart was pounding. His strength was ebbing fast.

Then he heard the roar of a motorboat in the distance. But it was impossible to wave his free arm and still hold up Will Barrow. His mind began to

Barrow were being pulled into a boat

blur, and the next thing Tom knew, he and Will were being pulled into a boat. Soon after, other arms were helping them ashore, amid cheers and congratulations from the men. Then two jeeps came speeding up to rush Tom and Will off to the island's infirmary.

A half hour later, wrapped in a blanket, Tom sat up on his cot. He drank piping-hot cocoa with Bud and Hank. Will Barrow had been ordered to bed by Dr. Carman, the physician at Fearing Island, to recuperate from his ordeal. Tom, however, seemed to have come through with no ill effects.

"I'd sure like to know what caused that tidal wave," the young inventor mused. "Somehow I have a hunch that it was man-made."

"Take a bow, chum. Your hunch is right," Bud replied bitterly. "The control-tower operator saw a plane hovering over the water just before it happened."

"So that's it!" Tom snapped his fingers. "Then the pilot must have dropped a bomb!"

Bud nodded. "It figures, all right."

"There's some more bad news you haven't heard yet, Tom," put in Hank Sterling reluctantly. "That rocket you sent up was swept off the beach by the waves. Right now, it's lying some place at the bottom of the channel."

Without hesitation Tom replied, "Hank, order a salvage tug to get on the job and send down a diver."

"Right away, skipper." But before he left, Hank

leaned forward and put his hand on the boy's shoulder. "Listen to me, Tom," he urged. "From now on, take my advice and watch your step—every move you make! This is the third attack against you, not to mention those two warnings you got. Next time you may not get off so lucky!"

Bud added a word of caution to Hank's suggestion, and Tom promised to heed the advice. But he pointed out soberly:

"The trouble is, these attacks aren't the kind you can guard against. Take that guided missile, for instance, or the blast they touched off when we were hunting for the launching site. How could we forestall those, any more than we could forestall what happened today?"

Hank admitted the truth of this, adding, "Even so, that's another good reason for being extra careful!"

"You're right as usual, Hank," Tom said thoughtfully. "And there's one thing I can do right away."

After changing into dry clothes, he headed for the communications room, accompanied by Bud. "Where to now, pal?"

"The Florida police are working with the FBI in checking on that fellow Horton," Tom explained. "I'll call them and see what they've turned up. It may give us a clue to whatever else is being planned against us."

A few moments later he was talking by long-distance to the captain at Key West.

"This may surprise you," the police official reported, "but Major Horton is definitely in the clear. The FBI checked his records and we've investigated every move he's made here in Florida. Horton is above suspicion of any subversive activity—even holds a Silver Star for gallantry. And we find nothing to indicate that he has any grudge against you or your father."

"That certainly is a surprise!" Tom exclaimed.

"Here's something else that may interest you," the captain went on. "When Horton winds up his vacation, he plans to apply for a job in rocketry."

Tom was amazed. An idea came to him. "Look, Chief," he said. "If the FBI is sure Horton is trustworthy, send him to Shopton for an interview. We're looking for good rocket men ourselves."

After completing the call, Tom told Bud about the strange turn of events. But his friend was strongly opposed to the idea of inviting Horton to take part in their new project.

"You can't tell me that two guys with a short great toe would have been on that Florida beach at the same time!" Bud protested. "That would be too much of a coincidence."

Tom assured Bud that Horton would be thoroughly screened again at Shopton, then he changed the subject. He reminded Bud that they had not yet translated the message from outer space. By telephone he ordered a copy of his father's space dictionary flown from Swift Enterprises.

It was delivered by a shuttle plane early in the evening, and Tom settled down in the room he shared with Bud to translate the symbols he had copied off the oscilloscope earlier that day. Bud looked on with keen interest while his friend decoded the message.

"Well, what does it say?" Bud asked eagerly, when the young scientist looked up from his task.

"Assuming my translation is correct," Tom replied, "this message tells us that our space friends live on an artificial satellite of the planet Mars."

"An artificial satellite! You mean some kind of a space station they've built?"

"Right. And they use it as a base for manufacturing space rockets. After that, the message goes on to invite us to do something."

"Do what?" Bud asked curiously.

Tom shook his head. "Unfortunately, that's where the message petered out. The machine went dead right at that point."

"Oh, fine!" Bud said impatiently. "Then we won't have any idea what they were trying to tell us until the next message comes through. And that may not be for weeks!"

"I didn't say I had no idea," Tom corrected. "In fact, I believe I *know* what they were trying to say."

CHAPTER 10

A VOLTAGE VICTORY

BUD STARED at his friend in surprise. "Don't keep me in suspense, genius boy!" he pleaded. "Come on! What's the news from the Martian space station?"

"You remember some of those earlier messages our friends out there sent us?" Tom asked.

"Sure. They wanted to visit the earth but couldn't figure out how to survive in our atmosphere— wasn't that the general idea?"

"Right! But they never were able to describe themselves well enough for Dad and me to form any idea of what their bodies are like."

Bud grinned. "They may be bugs or fish or something really out of this world?"

"Correct. So naturally we couldn't give them any advice."

"What's on their minds now?" Bud asked.

"I have a hunch they've given up on that angle for the time being, and now they want *us* to come and visit *them*."

"Say! How about that?" Bud exclaimed, reacting with wide-eyed interest. "Man, a trip like that would suit me!"

"Me too," Tom agreed. "And another thing— visiting their satellite would be simpler than visiting Mars itself, because we wouldn't have any poisonous atmosphere to contend with."

"Okay, you've convinced me!" Bud said enthusiastically. "How soon do we start?"

Tom laughed. "Slow down, fly boy! A space station is still the first step in conquering interplanetary space. Besides, even a trip to a Martian satellite would take a little too long now for my taste."

"How long?" queried Bud.

Tom thought for a moment. "The round trip would take over two and a half years at the rate of speed our rockets can go now."

Bud's face fell as Tom added, "And almost half that time would be spent waiting for the right moment to take off on our return trip."

"Well, there goes a dream—with a dull thud," Bud commented glumly.

"Don't take it so hard." Tom chuckled. "We'll beat that speed problem yet. In the meantime, if those Martians can travel faster than we can in our rockets, maybe they'll come to visit our space station. I'll send a message that we're planning to build one."

Using the space dictionary, Tom began working out a formula that would convey this idea to his space friends. Later, he would beam the message to their satellite by powerful radio impulses.

Bud went to bed. Long after midnight he awakened in his bunk to see Tom still working.

"Jumpin' jets!" he gasped, rubbing his eyes sleepily. "Are you still at it?"

Tom looked up with a rueful grin. "This job's tougher than I realized," he admitted. "I'll need symbols we don't even have in our space dictionary."

"Better put it away and get some shut-eye," Bud advised, "or you'll be going around snoring on your feet tomorrow."

Tom yawned and stretched, then pushed back his chair. "Guess you're right," he sighed. "I believe I'll have to call on Dad for help."

The next day Tom was working in his laboratory on some new rocket refinements when the phone rang. "Tom Swift," he answered, leaning over to lift the instrument toward him.

"Hank Sterling, Tom. The salvage tug just raised your experimental rocket. Want to come to the beach and examine it, or shall we haul it up to your lab?"

"Bring it here, please," Tom said eagerly.

As the young inventor waited, a tractor rolled up

outside the laboratory. Cradled in a carriage hooked on behind was the rocket, which workmen quickly transferred to a test stand inside the building.

To Tom's relief, the rocket appeared unharmed by its immersion in salt water, and the battery inside was still intact. Word of the successful salvage operation had spread like wildfire over the island, and a number of engineers and technicians had gathered to watch the test. Among them were Bud, Hank, and George Dilling.

Working swiftly, Tom plugged several rubber-insulated leads into a big control board, and connected two more to the solar-battery terminals. Then, his heart thumping, he stepped back to the board and closed a switch. Instantly the voltmeter needle swung around to the right, then kept moving farther and farther around the dial.

"Wow! Look at that!" Bud cried.

When the needle finally came to rest, the onlookers could hardly believe their eyes. Tom himself gave a whistle of amazement.

"Hang on to your space hats!" cried the young inventor with a broad smile. "That voltage is almost fifty percent higher than I'd hoped for. Why, each cell tests better than two hundred volts and it will be easy to make batteries with line voltage of a thousand or more."

Bud gave a whoop of triumph and pumped his friend's hand up and down, as the others added their congratulations.

"Tom, this is the greatest job of research and development you've ever done," George Dilling said. "It may revolutionize the whole power industry!"

"It could—*if* the battery holds its charge properly," Tom said, checking his own enthusiasm. "I'd better give it an aging test before we start counting our orders!"

Tom spent the rest of the afternoon rigging up a special test chamber. Inside it, the battery would be connected to a heavily overloaded circuit and at the same time undergo extreme conditions of temperature, pressure, and electrical stress.

"What's all this supposed to prove?" Bud queried.

"It'll show how well the desensitizer can do its job," Tom explained. "Twelve hours in this chamber will drain the battery as much as six months of normal use would. If that voltage needle points anywhere near as high tomorrow as it does right now, we'll know we've got something!"

After breakfast the next morning, the two boys hurried to the laboratory. By this time, the battery had undergone almost fifteen hours of testing. Tom removed it from the chamber and quickly hooked up the leads for another reading. To his delight, the voltage had dropped only a minute fraction of one percent!

Tom was jubilant. "Bud, this means the battery has a terrific efficiency! It should last for years—and you've seen how lightweight it is. It's just what we need for powering all the equipment at our outpost in space!"

"Okay, then," said Bud enthusiastically, "if you've got your battery perfected, what's to stop us from building the space station right now?"

"Nothing," Tom said. "At least not from building the kind that rotates to create artificial gravity. But I'm still hoping that the crew can live without gravity in a nonspinning type. So our next problem to work on is that Zero-G chamber I told you about."

"The heliplane will be waiting without, sir," Bud quipped, saluting.

The boys took off shortly and flew back to Enterprises with Hank Sterling. Tom radioed ahead and instructed Miss Trent to arrange a meeting with Ned Newton for two thirty that afternoon at Tom's office. Mr. Newton arrived promptly.

"Hi, Uncle Ned! Good to see you again!" Tom said, shaking hands with the dark, rather dignified man and offering him a chair.

"I hear that you had an exciting time on Fearing Island," Uncle Ned remarked, as he settled himself in one of the deep leather chairs.

"We sure did." Tom grinned. "And I think we have some pretty exciting results to show for it." He handed over the solar battery, which he had brought back in the heliplane. Uncle Ned examined it with interest.

"Tom, if this new invention of yours is half as useful as your preliminary report indicated, it should find quite a market."

"You be the judge, Uncle Ned," Tom said, brimming with confidence. "A battery one-tenth the size of this will provide enough energy to run an automobile for the life of the car. On the other hand, we can easily make one big enough to power an ocean liner."

"Incredible!" Mr. Newton said, as Tom continued:

"But that's not all. These solar batteries will find particular application wherever the weight factor is all-important, as in aircraft and rocketry. And how about pocket-sized arc welders and dentists' drills?

"What about the cost?" Uncle Ned interjected.

"They'll be high-priced to start with," Tom admitted. "But in terms of long life, they may well turn out to be the cheapest form of power known."

"But look here," put in Uncle Ned. "Consider the expense of sending cargo rockets back and forth to charge up the batteries with solar power. Wouldn't it be cheaper to manufacture them at your space station and then send them down to earth?"

"That's what I'm planning on—two complete factories at my outpost."

The discussion continued for a while longer, with Mr. Newton becoming more and more enthusiastic. When he finally rose to go, he clapped the young scientist on the shoulder and remarked:

"Profitwise, Tom, you've really surpassed yourself! A year from now, I shouldn't be surprised if your solar batteries turned out to be our biggest product!"

After Uncle Ned had left, the intercom buzzed. "A Mr. Kenneth Horton is at the outer gate," Miss Trent reported. "He claims that you invited him here, and the watchman wants to know whether to admit him."

"Thank you. I'll take care of it." Tom called the gatehouse. "Have you checked Horton's credentials?"

"Yes," the watchman replied. "He showed me his Army discharge papers, a copy of his birth certificate, and a security clearance from the FBI with his picture on it. They all seem to be in good order."

"All right," said Tom. "Give him an electronic amulet and send him over to my office."

Special amulets, worn on bracelets, were given to all authorized personnel and visitors. They served to trap radar impulses, which otherwise would show up as blips on the radarscopes used to detect intruders.

Tom had just clicked off the intercom when the red signal flashed on the TV control board. Hurrying over, he switched on the videophone. The face of Kane, the Florida telecaster, came into view on the screen. His voice was urgent.

"Tom, have you hired that fellow Horton yet?"

"No."

"Then don't take him on," said Kane. "I just had a warning that he is a foreign agent."

Tom was thunderstruck. "Who sent it?"

"I don't know. It was marked top secret, but the message was unsigned." Kane held the paper up for Tom to scrutinize on the screen.

"All right. Thanks for letting me know," Tom said in a troubled voice.

As Kane signed off, Chow Winkler strolled into the office, his sun-bronzed face wreathed in a grin. "Tom, you gonna be wantin' a bite to eat here at the plant this evenin'?" he asked. "If you are, I'd like to fix somethin' a mite special."

Tom hardly heard him. He was thinking about the disturbing news that he had just received from Kane. But he answered, "Thanks, Chow, but I'll probably be shoving off at five o'clock." Then, as the cook turned to leave, Tom added abruptly, "Say, wait a minute!"

A sudden idea had struck the puzzled young inventor. Time and again, Tom had noticed that Chow had a natural gift for character reading. Explaining that he was about to receive a caller, Tom said, "Stay around, Chow, and look the man over. Then later on tell me what you think of him."

The Texan agreed, greatly pleased by this mark of confidence in his shrewdness. A few seconds later Miss Trent ushered Horton into the office. Tom glanced at Chow to catch his first reaction. To his surprise, the cook's jaw had dropped open in a look of utter amazement!

CHAPTER 11

AMAZING NEWS

CHOW'S UNMISTAKABLE RECOGNITION of Kenneth Horton startled Tom. Was the ex-major friend or foe? Tom found out a second later when Horton exploded with:

"Chow Winkler, you old bean wrangler!"

The two men rushed together in a bear hug, then pumped hands and clapped each other joyfully on the back.

"Brand me for a three-toed bronc if you ain't a sight for sore eyes!" cried Chow, holding Horton at arm's length to look at him. "Where'd you come from, boy?"

The caller quickly told about vacationing in Florida after his discharge from the Army, and how he had received an invitation to come to Swift Enterprises for an interview.

"Brand my fuselage!" the cook exclaimed, remembering Tom's request. "I almost forgot what I'm doin'! Tom, I've knowed Kenny Horton here since he was knee-high to a horny toad. I used to work for his pa on the ole Lazy H spread, down in the Panhandle. You take it from me, Tom, you can bank on anything this young feller says or does, 'cause they ain't no finer folks exist than the Hortons from Texas!"

It was Kenneth Horton's turn to be puzzled. "That sounds as if I were under suspicion for some reason," he remarked quizzically.

"You were," Tom admitted. "But in view of what Chow tells me, I'm sure we can forget all that."

The young inventor then proceeded to explain about the attacks on his life, the warning left in the pop bottle on the beach, and the tracks of the man with the short toe.

Ken Horton burst out laughing. "No wonder I was a prime suspect!" He chuckled. "But maybe I can still help you."

"How so?" Tom asked.

"I saw another man on the beach with the same kind of toe peculiarity."

Tom was startled by this revelation and asked for a description of the man.

"Well, he was dark-haired, slender, and about thirty years old," Horton replied. "Frankly, I didn't like him. He seemed a little oily. And he talked a lot, too. He struck up conversations with several people on the beach."

"I don't suppose you overheard anything that might give us a lead?" Tom asked.

Horton shook his head, then frowned. "Wait a minute! I do remember something. He was flirting with a girl and mentioned his name. Seems to me it was something ending in '—erman.'"

Tom excused himself and went to the videophone. He asked the operator to signal the Key West station, then waited until Kane's picture appeared on the screen. Tom relayed the information given him by Horton and requested Kane to pass it along to the police.

"Have them get in touch with me the minute they turn up any lead," he added before signing off.

"Roger!"

When Tom rejoined Chow and Horton, the cook wanted to know whether these developments might cause Tom to change his mind about leaving the plant at five o'clock.

"They might at that," Tom admitted. Turning to Horton, he asked, "How about having dinner with me here? Chow can fix something."

"Glad to," said the former Army officer. "That'll give me plenty of time to talk about several ideas I have."

Chow beamed. "I'll whip up the best-tastin' mess o' Western vittles you ever et!"

"Sounds good to me," Horton said, smiling.

"Suppose we make it the lounge of the main lab," Tom suggested. As Chow went out the door, Tom called after him with a chuckle, "Only don't serve any stewed rattlesnake with cactus dressing!"

When Chow had gone, Horton said, "I had no idea I was under suspicion. But now that I'm in the clear, what can I do for you?"

"Enterprises needs good rocket men, Ken, and you may fill the bill. Is it true that you're interested in space travel?"

When Horton replied that he was intensely interested, Tom went on to question him about his technical background. Impressed by Horton's answers, Tom said cordially:

"Ken, I'd like very much to have you join our satellite program. With your Signal Corps experience, I believe you'd make a good liaison man between Swift Enterprises and the broadcasting companies who are interested in our project."

Tom described the undertaking in more detail, adding, "Of course you'd have to pass certain tests first in order to qualify for any trips into space. And I warn you, they're rugged!"

Horton was excited by the daring plan to establish an outpost in space. "I'd give my right arm to get in on a project like that!" he exclaimed. "How soon may I take those tests?"

Pleased by Horton's eagerness, Tom called Bud Barclay on the plant telephone. "Drop around to my office as soon as you can. I have a new candidate for your torture chambers!"

Bud replied with a mock fiendish chuckle. "Be

over as fast as I can hop on my jet-propelled broom. Don't let him get away!"

A few moments later Bud strode into the office. But upon being introduced to Horton, the affable grin on his face suddenly chilled.

Tom quickly dispelled his friend's anxiety. "You can turn off the deep freeze, chum," he said. "We have Chow's personal assurance that our guest is okay."

After hearing Tom's explanation about the man's background and the second person on the beach with a short great toe, Bud finally thawed out. "Sorry I behaved like a chump," he apologized. "But after what's happened, I wasn't feeling very friendly toward the guy who made those footprints in the sand."

"I don't blame you," Horton said. "In your place, I'd have been suspicious, too—and would be until that other chap is found."

"Think you want to trust yourself in my hands on those space tests?" Bud asked, grinning.

"Lead the way, pardner. Open the chute and let 'er rip!"

While the tests were going on, Tom went to check on his Zero-G project, and was pleased to learn that it would be ready for him to try out the next day. Then he returned to his office.

It was after five o'clock when Kenneth Horton got back. He dropped into a chair.

"How'd you make out?" Tom asked him.

"You weren't kidding. Those space tests *are* rugged!" Horton laughed. "But I'm still on two feet and your pal seems to think I'll do."

"Congratulations! I'll call Chow and tell him we're ready to eat."

After putting through the call to Chow, Tom drove his new recruit to the three-story laboratory building. He beamed his electronic key at the entrance and a sliding steel door rose to admit the jeep to an automatic lift shaft. Tom drove inside, flicking another combination with his key. The lift rose to the second floor. A conveyor belt then carried the jeep down the plant wing to an automatic parker at the door of the lounge.

Ken Horton expressed his amazement at everything he had seen that afternoon. "Tom, this is like walking into a whole new world of scientific wonders!" he commented.

A short time later Chow arrived, wheeling a stainless-steel serving cart. It was loaded with steaming dishes that gave off an appetizing aroma.

The former range cook chuckled. "Never thought you'd see me drivin' this kind of a chuck wagon back on the Lazy H, did you, Ken boy?"

"No. But from the smell of that food, I can see you've lost none of your old touch with a skillet!"

Chow had indeed prepared a feast. As Tom and Ken plunged into the tempting array of Western ranch dishes, including steak and tortillas, Chow looked on, beaming at their evident enjoyment.

While the cook was clearing away the dessert dishes, a call on the public-address system summoned Tom to the wall phone. When he answered, a long-distance operator connected him with the chief of police at Key West.

"Your tip paid off in a hurry," the officer announced. "We have the short-toed man who left those prints on the beach!"

CHAPTER 12

HUMAN FLY!

THE SPEED of the police work amazed Tom. "Congratulations, Captain!" he exclaimed. "How did you find the suspect?"

"I'd call it a lucky break," the officer replied. "We checked the hotel guest lists for names ending in 'erman,' and nailed the right man almost immediately. A desk clerk pointed him out to one of my detectives just as he was coming back from a swim. His name, by the way, is Eli K. Rhoderman."

"How about the description?" Tom asked.

"It fits, all right. He's thirty-one years old, dark-haired, five feet nine, and weighs a hundred and thirty-seven pounds. Says he's a traveling salesman for the Quik Battery Corporation."

"The Quik Battery Corporation!" Tom echoed.

"That name mean something to you?" asked the captain.

"It sure does! Quik is working on a new product similar to one I'm developing. The president of the company already has tried to make trouble for me in court. Is Rhoderman with you now?"

"In the next office," the police captain replied. "Suppose I put him on the extension phone for a three-way talk."

"Good idea!"

A moment later Tom heard the click of a receiver being lifted. A shrill, angry voice began to pour out a flood of indignant complaints.

"Take it easy, Mr. Rhoderman," Tom said in a mild voice. "You haven't been charged with anything so far."

"Then what's the idea of having me arrested?" stormed the salesman.

"You haven't been arrested yet," the captain's voice broke in. "You were merely brought here for questioning and I advise you to cooperate for your own good."

"I've already answered your questions," retorted Rhoderman. "What else do you want to know?"

"Someone threatened me in an unsigned note," said Tom. "The note was left in a pop bottle on the beach. Can you explain how the footprints leading away from it happen to match yours?"

"No, and I don't propose to try. I dare say I've left my prints all over the beach since I've been here. If that's the only evidence you have against me, better pull in your horns!"

"We will need more evidence to hold Mr. Rhoderman," the captain admitted, none too happily.

Tom asked Rhoderman several other pertinent questions, hoping to catch him off guard or perhaps link him in some way with the attack on Kane. But the salesman parried all questions cleverly, without revealing any useful information.

Finally Tom said, "All right, I guess there's no use pressing the matter any further."

"That means you're free to go, Rhoderman," the captain growled.

"Thanks for nothing!" jeered the suspect. Tom heard him slam down the phone.

"I'm convinced that he's our man," commented the captain. "We'll put a tail on him when he leaves here, and I'll let you know if he tries any funny business."

Tom thanked the officer for his prompt and efficient handling of the case, then hung up. When Horton heard the story, he was glad to learn that Rhoderman would be shadowed. The two new friends talked for a couple of hours, before they parted for the night.

The next morning Tom's whole family accompanied him to the plant to witness his first test of the Zero-G chamber. Phyl Newton and Ken Horton also came along.

Bud Barclay greeted them in the main building. "All set for your act?" he asked Tom.

"I'd better be," Tom replied, leading the way to

the Zero-G chamber. "Looks as if I'm going to have a good-sized audience."

Chow Winkler and a number of engineers and other employees were already gathered around the test chamber. It was made of transparent plastic and was thirty feet square and fifteen high. On the ceiling was rigged one pole of a special electromagnet of Tom's design. Inside, the room had been furnished with a desk, chair, couch, and tools.

Dave Bogard, an electrical engineer employed by Swift Enterprises, was putting the final touches on the control panel which stood alongside the Zero-G chamber.

"How's she coming, Dave?" Tom asked him.

"When this panel was moved, one of the wires came loose. Kind of tricky the way you have these fine adjustments set up. I guess I'll have to consult the diagram."

He was referring to a system of supersensitive electronic controls. These had been designed to compensate for the slightest shift in position of any test object inside the chamber, whether human or otherwise. Thus the controls would maintain a precise balance at all times between the downward pull of gravity and the upward attraction of the magnet.

"Here, lend me your screw driver," Tom suggested, and soon wired the connections.

Dave shook his head and grinned admiringly. "I don't know how you do it, Tom, but you've sure got what it takes."

Tom lightly brushed the compliment aside. "After all, I drew the diagrams, so I *should* know how to make the hookup."

"Tom," Phyl asked, as she stared wide-eyed through the transparent plastic walls, "do you expect to overcome the law of gravity in there?"

"No. But I hope to imitate the helpless feeling one would have if he were weightless," Tom explained. "My body won't be weightless, although it will appear to be when I'm inside the chamber in a special suit made for the experiment. The buoyancy of my suit in the pulsating magnetic field will exactly compensate for the weight of my body."

Bud grinned and scratched his head. "I'll buy a return ticket," he said, "and if any of the rest of you think you understand this gimmick, you're entitled to a free pass to the booby hatch!"

Everyone laughed, but Sandy said, winking at her brother, "It's all very clear to me. Where's this suit that you're going to wear, Tom? Mother and I want to be sure it fits right."

Tom winked. "It's the latest fashion on Mars," he said. "If you'll excuse me, I'll go put it on."

Tom returned in a few minutes. His appearance drew a loud buzz of interest. From head to foot, he was clothed in a weird, tight-fitting metal suit resembling fish scales. Slits had been left for his eyes, ears, and nose.

The suit had been tailored especially for Tom and was made like a bulletproof jacket. It was composed of a myriad of tiny soft iron disks, sewn together on a fabric backing. The disks were built up like the flesh on his frame, clustering most heavily on the thickest parts of his body, whereas the gloves encasing his hands were fairly thin.

"Well, brand my lariat, a walkin' hardware store!" Chow exclaimed. "How can you ever move around in that there suit o' armor?"

"Feels a bit heavy, all right." Tom chuckled. "But I'm expecting the Zero-G chamber to change all that."

Mrs. Swift laid a hand on her son's arm. "Tom, there—there's nothing dangerous about this experiment, is there?" she asked anxiously.

Tom patted her hand before replying. "Well, Mother, I'm not going to electrocute myself, if that's what you mean. But if I should feel any bad reaction, I'll signal Dad to turn off the power immediately."

"Good luck, Tom," said Mr. Swift. He stepped to the control board as prearranged.

Tom entered Zero-G chamber and closed the door behind him, then signaled his father to turn on the current. Now he was sealed in the air-conditioned chamber!

Tom experienced a queer sensation of buoyancy and lightness. He tried to take a step. To his surprise, the upward motion lifted him gently off the floor. Now he hung suspended in mid-air.

"I think I know how to get out of this," Tom said

to himself. Tilting his head back, he somersaulted. The force shoved him back to the floor again.

Tom realized at once that he would have to master a new gait. Shuffling his feet along the floor, he dragged his body behind like a comedian doing a funny act. His audience laughed uproariously at the strange antics.

Even Tom had to grin at his predicament. "Wait till they see this one." Standing on tiptoes, he gave a bound to the ceiling, where he walked on his hands! Then, pushing with his fingers, he made his way to one of the walls, which he crept down on hands and knees.

By now Tom realized the importance of his Zero-G chamber. It would be far too costly to train spacemen in zero gravity, involving many hours flying around the earth in rockets. His crew could learn the fundamental movements of overcoming weightlessness right in the Zero-G chamber.

Tom's tension was vanishing, and he resolved to make his experiment real fun. He propelled himself toward one side of the room and proceeded to walk straight up the wall!

Startled gasps broke from the audience. "Tom Swift the Human Fly!" Bud exclaimed.

The cries of amazement grew louder as Tom continued his stroll by walking upside down across the ceiling!

Chow Winkler yanked out a red bandanna and mopped his brow nervously as he stared in horrified

"Tom Swift the Human Fly!" Bud exclaimed

fascination. "Brand my Damonscope," he exclaimed, "that ain't human! How's Tom ever goin' to know which is top side up when he comes out o' that place?"

Reaching the other side of the room, Tom calmly walked down the wall. Next, he lay down on the couch. His body, being buoyant, failed to dent the cushions. And because he lay without exerting any energy, he was gradually propelled off the couch and left floating in the center of the room.

Tom now turned his attention to some of the other equipment in the room. When he sat at the desk and wrote, even the slight effort of wielding a pencil caused him to be shoved backward against his chair.

The tools and other items in the room had been made specially for the experiment. They contained just enough iron to counterbalance the pull of gravity. A slight touch was enough to send a wrench or wastebasket floating across the room!

Finally Tom picked up a hammer and tried to drive a nail into a board. As he swung the hammer downward, his feet shot up from the floor and the hammer landed feebly on the nail. "I never felt so helpless in my life," Tom murmured.

The observers outside Zero-G chamber were laughing and talking with great interest as they watched Tom's every move. At last they saw him straighten up and signal to his father that the experiment was over.

Smiling and pleased at the outcome, Mr. Swift reached toward the control board. But the smile suddenly faded. The switch refused to budge—it was locked in the "on" position!

Mr. Swift gave a harder yank. Still the switch would not move. Bud came over to lend a hand. Even between them, they could not budge it!

"The controls have frozen!" Bud whispered, his heart sinking. Sensing that something was wrong, the rest of the audience pressed closer.

Tom wondered what had happened, but did not speak, knowing that his voice could not be heard through the soundproof walls. And the door could not be opened until the current was turned off!

A look of alarm came over the faces of Mrs. Swift and the girls. They recalled Tom's remarks about the possible danger of space sickness. What if he should suffer the effects of overexposure before he could be freed from the chamber!

But as Dave Bogard stepped forward to offer assistance, Mr. Swift noticed a blue light beam aimed at the main control switch.

"That son of mine!" He chuckled, unlocking a hidden safety device. "He thinks of everything. Only he should have told me about this!"

Tom emerged from the test chamber to face an excited hail of comments, questions, and congratulations.

"Do you think a space crew will be able to adjust all right to zero gravity?" Horton asked eagerly.

"I'm sure of it, Ken," Tom replied. "But we'll all need careful training to develop a new set of reflexes for weightlessness. I think we can learn them in the Zero-G chamber, but to be sure, I'm going up in space to make a check test."

The young inventor decided on an orbit 350 miles above the earth. He took off a week later from Fearing Island.

As the rocket arrowed upward and each booster stage was released for a fresh burst of power, Tom was pushed hard against the acceleration couch by the force of many G's. But he did not feel the force too severely. A gravitational device he had invented for the rocket in which he and Bud had gone around the world reduced the pressure considerably.

The unpleasant sensation eased off as the rocket curved into its final orbit. The flight tape acted automatically to cut the motors. In a silent world of space, the ship was now racing around the earth at almost 17,000 miles an hour!

Tom unhooked his safety belt and promptly floated out into the center of the cabin. He was now completely weightless!

During the rest of the flight, Tom carried out a variety of experiments. He tried eating, drinking, relaxing, and working with various tools. All the while he compared his reactions with the effects that he had noted in the Zero-G chamber.

"This is just about the same as that helpless feeling I got during my test," he said to himself elatedly, and practiced propelling his body forward and backward to accomplish various tasks.

When the rocket landed on Fearing Island, Bud, Hank Sterling, Horton, and a crowd of technicians were waiting to greet him.

"Boy, am I glad to see you back!" said Bud. "And not all battered up, either."

"How does it feel to go floating around like a feather up there?" Hank questioned.

"It's fun, once you get your bearings," Tom replied. "With proper training in our Zero-G chamber, a well-picked space crew should have no trouble at all learning what to do. But each man will need a metal suit tailored to his figure."

With a feeling of elation, Tom, Bud, and Hank took off in the heliplane for Swift Enterprises. Tom informed his companions that he was now ready to plunge forward in high gear on his space station project.

"What's this thing going to cost?" Bud asked. "And have the broadcasting companies agreed to share it?"

A strange look came over Tom's face. Then he admitted that he had completely forgotten this important detail!

Hank chuckled. "That's an inventor's privilege, I guess."

At the plant the next day Tom called John Reed,

the financial coordinator for Swift Enterprises. "Are the estimates in from all departments yet on our space station project, John?" he asked.

"Yes, the figures are all assembled, Tom: I'll send them right over. But I warn you—you're in for a shock!"

When Tom read the figures, a sinking feeling engulfed him. He sat in his office for hours, mulling over them. The total cost of the project on paper was staggering—far above his wildest estimate.

How would the broadcasting companies react to the colossal sum that would be their share? Would they still want to finance their part of the venture? Troubled, Tom telephoned William Bruce at the Consolidated Broadcasting Network in New York and asked him to arrange a conference within the next few days.

At seven, as he was leaving, Tom met Bud Barclay at the main gate. "No car?" Bud asked.

"Tonight I feel like walking. I've got a lot on my mind." Quickly he gave his friend the highlights.

Bud whistled and said kindly, "You aren't walking alone. We'll talk it over. In case you don't realize it, genius boy, you're too valuable to this setup to go wandering along dark roads by yourself at night!"

"Okay." Tom laughed. "You chaperon me to the house and we'll put you up overnight."

"It's a deal. My red convertible's due for a valve-grinding job. We'll leave it down at the Ace Garage and then walk the rest of the way."

After they left the car at the garage, the boys chose a short cut that led along South Bay Street. It was a dingy, run-down area, composed mainly of warehouses and shops of cheap wholesale merchants. The street was poorly lighted, with long patches of darkness between the few street lamps.

Suddenly Bud stopped short with a puzzled look. "Listen!" he commanded.

"What's the matter?" Tom asked.

"I thought I heard a car stopping in that alleyway up ahead. Since I'm looking out for you—"

Tom chuckled. "Probably a truck unloading in back of a store."

Nevertheless, the boys kept their eyes alert as they walked on. The entrance to the alley was too dark to make out anything, but all seemed quiet.

The two friends continued on their way, but a moment later Bud thought he heard soft footsteps behind them. Alarmed, he grabbed Tom's arm. Before they could turn around, heavy, crushing blows rained down on their heads!

Tom and Bud toppled to the pavement, unconscious!

CHAPTER 13

A CLOSE VOTE

AT THE SWIFT HOME, worry mounted with every passing hour as Tom failed to appear.

Sandy and her parents waited tensely in the living room. Again and again they telephoned various places, hoping to locate the missing youth. But every call drew a blank.

"Try the plant once again, dear," Mrs. Swift suggested to her husband as it neared ten o'clock.

The elder inventor went into the phone alcove and dialed. When he returned, his face was graver than ever.

"No luck," he announced. "But I did find out one thing. Tom was seen leaving the main gate with Bud Barclay around seven in Bud's car. They were going to a garage."

Mrs. Swift sobbed softly and Sandy put an arm around her mother's shoulder to comfort her. "What

are you going to do?" she called after her father as he
turned to leave the room.

"What I should have done long ago—get hold of
Harlan Ames!"

When reached by telephone, the security chief
promised to start a search at once. He would pick up
Mr. Swift and Phil Radnor. A short time later the
three men drove to the experimental station.

"We'll try to pick up their trail at the main gate,"
Ames said.

The job of tracking the boys' movements proved
slow and tedious. The searchers questioned attend-
ants at garage after garage before they found the
right one. But at Ace the nightman could not say
where the missing boys had gone.

Suddenly Mr. Swift snapped his fingers. "I just
remembered a short cut Tom sometimes takes on
his way home from downtown Shopton," he said.
"Let's try South Bay Street."

Ames cruised slowly along the dimly lighted street
while Radnor and Mr. Swift each played a searchlight along the sidewalks.

Suddenly Phil Radnor cried out, "There they
are!"

Ames swerved the car sharply to the curb and the
others leaped out. Tom and Bud were sprawled face
downward, inside an alleyway. Their heads sagged as
Mr. Swift and Radnor lifted them by the shoulders.

"No use trying to bring them to here. They need
a doctor," Ames said, running up.

The men's faces were grim and tight-lipped as they lifted the unconscious victims into the car. Ames raced to the Swift home, where Tom and Bud were put to bed and a doctor summoned immediately. Before he arrived, however, the boys began to regain consciousness.

Both were groggy but managed to answer questions about the attack. "Whoever hit Bud and me took us by surprise," Tom mumbled. "We didn't see them."

When Dr. Emerson reached the house, he examined the boys carefully and treated their head injuries. "Slight concussions," he announced as he replaced his instruments in his black medical bag. "They'll have to remain quiet for several days."

Radnor and Ames, meanwhile, had gone back to South Bay Street. With flashlights they examined the alley carefully for clues. It was apparent that the boys had been dragged into it after a car had pulled out.

"A man got out on each side of the car," Ames muttered. "You can see their footprints leaving and coming back. They must be the ones who slugged the boys because—"

Suddenly he broke off and pounced on an object imbedded in the dirt directly on top of one of the footprints.

"What is it?" Radnor asked.

Ames held the object up to his flashlight, revealing a small resistor of the type used in electronic circuits. The two security men exchanged startled glances.

"You suppose one of the thugs dropped it?" asked Radnor.

"Must have, or it would have been crushed into the dirt in the traffic along this alley."

"That means they were scientists or technical men. At least one of them was."

Ames nodded. "Might have been that fellow Rhoderman from the Quik Battery Corporation, trying to get even with Tom for having the police pick him up in Florida. Or, it could have been one of those foreign agents who fired the guided missile."

"What now, chief?"

"We'll take plaster impressions of these car tracks and footprints."

The next day Tom and Bud listened to Ames' report with keen interest. But the security chief told Tom that he had made no headway on the foreign angle and had been unable to locate Rhoderman to check the footprints. His company claimed that he was traveling on business and refused to reveal where.

"But one of these days," said Bud, "we'll find the guys, then just let me at 'em!"

The boys found their stay in bed highly irksome, in spite of Sandy and Mrs. Swift pampering them with attention. Phyl Newton made frequent visits, bringing fruit and books.

Tom spent much of his time working out the

message to his space friends, with help from his father. Chow Winkler dropped by one afternoon just as they added the last symbol to the communication.

The cook stared in amazement, then said, "What's that thing that looks like a bull?"

Before Tom could explain the meaning of the symbol, Bud said slyly to Chow, "Tom's space pals are having trouble roping a wild steer."

Chow grunted. He winked at the Swifts, but said to Bud with a straight face, "They musta et a patch o' loco weed. You can't trust one o' them locoed critters on earth *or* in the sky!" Tom and Mr. Swift burst out laughing and Bud finally grinned sheepishly.

Mr. Swift later sent off the message, urging that the men on the Martian satellite repeat their request.

By the end of the week, Dr. Emerson pronounced Tom and Bud entirely recovered. On Monday, Tom, his father, and Ken Horton met with the broadcasting group in the Swifts' office.

"Do you have an estimate ready for us?" Mr. Bruce asked eagerly.

Tom pulled down a chart on the wall. "I have the figures right here. They're broken down, so you can see how much each part of the project will cost."

By presenting the figures bit by bit, Tom hoped to soften the shock. But even so, he could see by the visitors' faces that they were taken aback by the tremendous over-all cost.

Mr. Paul Grunther, a heavy-set, balding executive, cleared his throat and commented with a frown, "Frankly, this figure is much higher than I expected. I'm not sure that my company will approve." There were murmurs of agreement. The broadcasters began to discuss the matter pro and con.

Listening to their remarks, Tom began to feel somewhat discouraged. Unless he could rouse their enthusiasm all over again, the project might be doomed! "Gentlemen," he put in, as an idea came to him, "I'd like to show you a completed model of the space station while you're thinking over the matter."

Opening a large cabinet, he held up the gleaming silver model of the wheel-shaped satellite. Tom went over each part of the design. He showed how the station would be constructed, with three sections carrying elaborate TV and radio antennae for picking up signals and beaming them back to earth.

Mr. Swift joined in, stressing the tremendous strides that radio communication could make with the help of a space station transmitter. He also emphasized the point that improvements in telecasting might boom the television industry so much that the project would pay for itself many times over.

Tom could see that some of the men were deeply impressed. But others still wore doubtful frowns. The young inventor exchanged glances with his father. It seemed as if nothing more could be done!

Tom was heartsick but would not admit defeat yet. In desperation, he decided to try one last bit of strategy—a written rather than a voiced vote, so no one would be swayed.

"Gentlemen, I suggest that in voting on the project, you each write Yes or No on a piece of paper without signing it."

"That sounds fair enough," Mr. Grunther admitted.

Tom handed out paper and pencils. He waited tensely as the men wrote their answers. Then he gathered the papers and read them aloud. Ken Horton kept score.

The result was eight to five in favor of going ahead. *Tom had won!*

"I'm glad the vote went this way," Mr. Bruce said.

After the committee had left, Mr. Swift put an arm around Tom's shoulders and congratulated him. "That was a masterful job. I admire the way you handled those men, son!"

"You really pulled this project out of the fire," added Horton. "Without that secret ballot, the vote might have been eight to five *against!*"

"Well, I'm pretty relieved," Tom admitted. "And now we can get to work in earnest."

"I think it's time for you to make a flight to Loonaui Island yourself, Tom," Mr. Swift suggested. "I'd like your opinion on the layout of the launching site. And you can start the natives working on the installation."

Tom was eager to go. Two days later he took off

for the Pacific in the *Sky Queen*. With him were
Bud, Ken Horton, and a crew of technicians. The
cargo deck of the Flying Lab was crammed with
equipment and supplies.

With its nuclear engines purring swiftly, the great
silver aircraft streaked across the continent faster
than the speed of sound. Soon they were soaring far
out above the broad Pacific.

Late that afternoon, Tom arrowed in for a landing on Loonaui. The lush tropical island was set like
a green jewel in the sparkling blue waters below.
Gentle rolling white breakers burst into foam
against the outlying coral reefs.

"Oh, man, I can feel that South Sea Island magic
already!" Bud sighed as he climbed out of the plane.

Tom and his friends were driven to the far end of
the island property which Mr. Swift had leased.
They were greeted by the native crew that Tom's father had engaged during his visit. A mammoth warehouse had already been constructed.

The natives were strong, sun-bronzed Polynesians.
Most of them were friendly, but one man in particular, named Pali, who spoke English, seemed different from the others, both in looks and disposition.
He wore a sulky, scowling expression. Tom noticed
that he seemed to be a man with a following.

"I wouldn't trust Pali farther than I could throw
a rocket," Bud confided later.

"Ditto," Tom agreed. "But I have no reason to

discharge him. If I do, it may only stir up trouble."

"Leave it to me," Bud said. "I'll keep an eye on him and find out if he's up to anything."

While Tom was busy setting up quarters for men and equipment that were to arrive from Shopton, Bud mingled casually with the natives. He soon realized that he could find out little without knowing the native language. Fortunately, Bud managed to make friends with a good-natured native boy, named Kipu, who agreed to act as translator.

Late that afternoon, Bud saw Pali and a group of friends stroll away from the work area. Summoning Kipu, he set out to trail them. Some distance away, he found the natives seated near a grass hut in a secluded grove of pandanus trees. Bud and Kipu crept up close enough to hear what was going on.

Pali was haranguing the other men in their native language. Suddenly Kipu clutched Bud's arm and turned to him with a look of terror.

"Come! We must go back to your friends at once! I fear trouble!"

CHAPTER 14

TERRIFIED NATIVES

TOM was checking cargo lists in his palm-thatched cottage when Bud and Kipu burst in.

"What's wrong?" Tom asked.

"We come to warn you!" cried Kipu, still wide-eyed with fear. "Pali is making great trouble. I heard him say you and the men with you are evil—that you come to shoot fire rockets at the sky. This will displease the spirits of nature. Pali tells the island people to destroy you or a great sickness will come to Loonaui!"

"Roarin' rockets!" Bud gasped. "What'll we do?"

"There's no sense getting all worked up," Tom advised.

"But you heard what he said!" Bud exclaimed.

"I'm not forgetting a word of it. But Dad had all those workers screened and I'm sure they're loyal."

"What about Pali? Would you call *him* loyal?"

"He's the one bad apple," Tom admitted. "But

if it comes to a showdown, the island police will prevent trouble."

Bud scowled uneasily. "I still think this setup is dangerous," he mumbled.

Tom went over to a crate of trade goods in the corner and took out some trinkets and bright-colored cloth, which he gave to Kipu.

"Here, take these for your kindness. You've done well to warn us about Pali. If you hear more news, come and tell us at once."

In the week that followed, there were no further signs of trouble. Tom threw all of his energy into the job of constructing the rocket base. Men and equipment arrived every day and work progressed rapidly. Soon a launching site was laid out.

Tom checked every bit of equipment carefully. Ken Horton, who had passed his Zero-G test, was intrigued by the weird-looking suits for the crew to wear while assembling the outpost in space. Made of tightly woven-wire fabric to withstand tremendous bursting pressure, the suits were coated with synthetic rubber both inside and out to make them absolutely airtight. The helmets were metal, with tinted transparent plastic visors to see through, and contained radio sets for talking back and forth with other crewmen.

"I'll sure feel like a being from another planet in one of these." Horton laughed. "Tell me more about them."

Tom explained that each suit would be provided

with its own oxygen supply and air-conditioning equipment.

"That's really necessary, isn't it?" Ken commented.

"It is, if we hope to survive any accidents out there in space," Tom replied.

"Such as?"

"Well, suppose a meteorite plowed a hole through one of the walls of the space station. All the air would rush out of that compartment, and the men who repaired the damage would have to work in a temporary vacuum. Without these space suits, they'd suffer explosive decompression."

"Yes," said Ken. "The air in their lungs would explode outward and the blood would boil in their veins! It's a horrible thought."

"That's why everything has to be figured out so carefully beforehand," Tom commented.

He now showed Ken the midget one-man rockets that he had designed for the project. Each one had a pair of jointed, robotlike arms, controlled from inside, for handling tools or manipulating objects in space. The crewmen would "fly" around in these midget rockets while constructing the outpost or doing any outside work.

"Do you mind if I try on one of the space suits?" Horton asked.

"Go ahead." Tom grinned. "You'll have to learn how to climb into one some time before we take off. Might as well be now."

He helped Ken don the strange-looking suit, then placed the helmet over his head and connected it to the fitting around his neck. Horton clumped around in the outfit with obvious delight. By gestures he indicated to Tom that he wished to go over to his living quarters and inspect himself in a mirror.

Chuckling, Tom went back to his inventory checkoff. A moment later he heard a bloodcurdling scream!

Tossing his clipboard aside, he dashed out of the hut. A fantastic sight met his eyes.

A native, popeyed with terror, had dropped to his knees in front of the weird-looking "spaceman." As Horton stood rooted to the spot, embarrassed and helpless, the native was salaaming up and down, screaming for mercy at the top of his lungs.

Before Tom could intervene, other natives rushed up and joined in the procedure. He tried vainly to stop them.

Tom let out a yell for Kipu, who came on the run. After quickly explaining what was happening, Tom said:

"Tell them it is just a special suit we need for our work. There's an ordinary man like ourselves inside! Make them understand it's all right!"

By this time a small mob of people had gathered. Kipu now shouted a stream of reassuring words in his native tongue. Then, with Tom's assistance, Horton took off his helmet and space suit.

Gradually the natives calmed down and straggled back to their various tasks. But in place of friendly smiles, their faces now wore expressions of distrust.

The terrified native was screaming for mercy

Bud was more worried than ever. "Listen, skipper," he warned, "you ought to screen every one of these natives again. Give them a lecture on what's happening, and then get rid of the guys who can't take it."

"Good idea," Tom agreed. Because of Horton's experience as a training instructor with Army recruits, Tom asked him to give the lecture, with Kipu acting as translator. "I'm sure that the men will gradually get used to the queer sights around here," he added.

Bud still did not share his friend's confidence. After lunch he and Ken Horton went with Tom to inspect the launching site. A small concrete blockhouse had been built. Technicians were busy installing electrical controls and instruments.

"Once the project starts, we'll be launching a rocket every day," Tom told his friends.

There would be twelve of them, each forming a "spoke" of the wheel-shaped space station. The spokes, shaped like tapered cylinders, would be the center section of the rocket fuselage during the flight to outer space. Upon reaching the orbit, these center sections would be removed and become part of the station. The other rockets would be conventional cargo types, loaded with supplies and equipment.

Later on, rockets would fly back and forth regularly between Loonaui Island and the outpost on a shuttle schedule.

Bud chuckled. "I can just hear that dispatcher's voice now. *Rocket leaving on platform nine!*"

After dark that evening the three friends decided to take time out for relaxation and pay a visit to the quaint trading village at the north end of the island.

Kipu came along in the jeep to act as translator.

The narrow, twisting dirt streets, poorly lighted with torches and oil lamps, were crowded with people. Natives in colorful wrap-around garments rubbed shoulders with planters in soiled white ducks and sailors from the trading schooners. The ships lay at anchor in the harbor.

Tom and his companions wandered from shop to shop, sampling native dishes, such as fish, poi, and yams. They also bought some wood carvings and dyed tapa cloth to take home as souvenirs for Mrs. Swift and the girls.

Suddenly Horton cried out, "It doesn't seem possible, but there's Rhoderman—that fellow I saw on the beach in Florida!"

CHAPTER 15

A PRISONER

RHODERMAN in Loonaui! Tom and Bud stiffened with excitement as Ken Horton pointed to a slender, dark-haired man lounging against the porch of a trading store.

"Are you sure that it's Rhoderman?" asked Tom tensely.

"Positive!" Ken replied.

Just then, Tom received a fresh shock. Another man stepped out of the crowd and joined Rhoderman. The newcomer was a powerful, apelike man in a striped seaman's jersey. He had long, thick arms and a brutal, heavy-jawed face—a face the young scientist would never forget!

"The Gorilla!" Tom gasped.

For the first time he had proof that the Quik Battery salesman was mixed up with the group that had fired the mysterious missile at him!

"Come on! Let's go get 'em!" Bud cried out.

The suspects heard him. Turning, they saw the boys and instantly darted down the street!

Tom and his companions took off in pursuit. But the slow-moving crowd of idlers in the crooked street forced them to weave in and out like broken-field runners in a football stadium.

"They went in there, I think!" shouted Horton, pointing to a squalid-looking restaurant.

The four pursuers dashed up on the porch and pushed their way inside through the beaded curtain that hung across the open doorway. The room was filled with the jangling music of a tinny piano and the chatter of sailors and natives.

When the portly Chinese owner bustled up, Tom asked him if he had seen the two men. "Solly! They no come in here!" replied the Chinese, shaking his head vigorously.

"Maybe we'd better look for ourselves!" snapped Bud.

Ignoring the owner's protests, Bud led the way as they plowed through the kitchen and back room, then emerged into an alleyway.

"We're out of luck!" Horton muttered.

Tom turned to ask Kipu to mingle with the islanders to learn if anyone had seen the two white men. But the native youth had disappeared!

For the next half hour, Tom and his friends combed the village, looking into shops and restaurants. But finally they gave up and returned to the spot where they had parked their jeep.

Tom was not upset, however. "Those men can't hide long on an island this size," he told the others. "I'll ask the police to post guards at the harbor and airfield to make sure that they don't get away."

Before Bud could start the jeep, a figure ran toward them from out of the darkness.

"It's Kipu!" Tom exclaimed.

The native boy was greatly excited and said that he had caught sight of the quarry just as Tom was entering the restaurant. Taking off on his own, he had trailed them to a deserted section of the beach.

"I saw them get into a boat—a fine motorboat!" Kipu reported. "Loonaui man run it. When I try to stop them, the white men point guns at me! Then they went away fast across the water!"

Tom asked Kipu to guide them to the spot on the beach. By the time they arrived, no ship lights were visible on the water.

"Any idea where they might be going?" Tom asked.

Kipu shrugged. "Maybe Moana. That is island east of here."

"How about our taking the *Sky Queen* up for a look, Tom?" Bud suggested. "We can use your dad's giant searchlight."

Tom snapped his fingers. "Let's go!"

Climbing back into the jeep, they sped off through the darkness on a winding dirt road to the island's airfield. A few moments later, with Tom at the controls, the huge Flying Lab took off, soaring seaward.

Bud went aft to the laboratory area and unlimbered the giant searchlight. This device, invented by Tom's father, was so powerful that it could illuminate vast areas with almost daylight brilliance.

Bud donned goggles to protect his eyes, then switched on the current. As the *Sky Queen* skimmed low over the water, he played the searchlight back and forth.

"We're on a wild-goose chase," Bud said over the intercom, after they had covered many square miles.

"Guess you're right," Tom agreed. "The motorboat must have ferried those two crooks to a seaplane."

"Which is probably high-tailing to the States," the copilot remarked, as Tom headed the big ship back toward the island. "Anyway, if they were here to bother you, Tom, I'm glad they're gone."

"We'll notify the FBI," said the young inventor.

As the *Sky Queen* neared the shore, its giant searchlight still illuminating the sea, Kipu exclaimed, "There's motorboat!"

Tom hovered low enough to get a good look at the sleek craft and its native pilot, who cowered under the blazing light.

"What'll we do now?" Bud asked excitedly.

"Let him go—for the moment," Tom replied. "Kipu can locate that fellow tomorrow."

Upon landing, Tom at once got in touch with the

Los Angeles office of the FBI. But when morning came, he received a report that Rhoderman had not landed anywhere on the West Coast.

After breakfast Tom sent Kipu to find the man who had operated the speedboat. The youth returned before lunchtime with the full story.

The native, named Ranui, had no connection with Rhoderman and the Gorilla. He worked for a wealthy planter, who owned the boat. The two strangers had asked him to take them out to the seaplane and he had done so.

"If Ranui's in the clear, Kipu," said Bud, "how come he didn't put up a squawk when those men pulled guns on you?"

"Ranui afraid I wanted to rob the men," Kipu explained.

That afternoon Tom contacted his father by short wave and reported the incident. "Sounds as though they're keeping a close watch on things," Mr. Swift commented. "I'll tell Harlan Ames. He and Radnor, as well as the police, are still working on the case. But they have no leads yet on the persons who fired that missile."

Tom also told his father that work on the rocket-launching base was going along well. After sending messages to his mother, Sandy, and Phyl, he signed off.

"There's one thing that still bothers me," mused Bud.

Tom slipped off the headphones. "What's that?"

"If those guys had to hire a boat to get out to their plane, how did they come ashore in the first place?"

Tom rubbed his chin thoughtfully. "You've got a point there. How about your going back to the village and see what you can find out?"

Bud agreed and set off in the jeep, after first depositing Tom at one of the warehouses. When Tom entered the big hut, he noticed that Pali was shifting some heavy bags containing the insulating material to be used in building the space station.

The tall, sullen-faced native had caused no trouble since the first evening and Kipu was of the opinion that he could now be trusted.

But Tom was curious to know what Pali was doing. "Why are you shifting those bags?" he asked.

Pali looked up affably and replied, "Many of your materials are becoming mildewed from the warm, damp climate. By stacking them this new way, the air will circulate better and help to keep them dry."

Tom noted with approval that he was now piling the bags in crisscross fashion, leaving the stack honeycombed with small air spaces.

"Good work, Pali! Thanks for changing them."

Tom walked away, puzzled by the man's unusually helpful attitude. He was also astounded to realize that Pali spoke excellent English.

After supper, while Tom was working alone in a laboratory he had set up, Pali approached him and said that there was something he would like to talk over with him in private. It was of a rather secret nature, he explained, so the two strolled away from the camp, side by side.

"No doubt you are surprised to learn that I am quite civilized after all," Pali began.

Tom shrugged. "I'll admit that I didn't know you spoke English so well."

Pali hesitated. "The fact is, I was not born on Loonaui. I have a great deal of white blood in me." He paused again and glanced at Tom, then blurted out, "I should like to join your space crew."

Tom was startled. He pointed out that all crew members would have to pass rigid tests and there was no equipment on the island for giving them.

"Very well, then," Pali persisted. "When you go back to the States, I should like to go along and take those tests."

Tom was more puzzled than ever. Pali seemed earnest. Moreover, he was well-built, athletic, obviously highly intelligent, and probably would make a good space crewman.

But Tom still felt uneasy. He had a hunch that Pali was up to something. Stalling for time, he said, "Frankly, I don't understand you, Pali. Aren't you happy here on Loonaui? You have no technical training. Why should you want to join my space crew?"

Pali laughed bitterly. "You say I have no training. Would it change your opinion if I told you that I once planned to be an engineer?"

Slowly Pali unfolded his story. A white relative had sent him to an American university. But he had been wild and reckless and had been expelled. Later he had drifted back to the islands.

As Pali talked, they reached a lonely stretch of beach. Palm trees straggled down to the water's edge. Tom noticed two native canoes tied together, drawn up on the sand.

Pali continued, "Now, perhaps, you will understand why I—"

He suddenly broke off with a sneering laugh as two natives sprang on Tom from behind, clapping a hand over his mouth. The young inventor twisted and fought but could not shake off his assailants.

"So—the brilliant young Tom Swift walks right into our trap." Pali chuckled. "They say experience is the only school for fools. But you will never have a chance to profit from this lesson."

His captors forced Tom down on the sand, then tied and gagged him. They quickly stripped off all his clothes but his shorts and half carried, half dragged him into one of the canoes. Both crafts were shoved into the water.

Leaping into the other canoe, the men paddled away from shore as fast as they could!

CHAPTER 16

ADRIFT AT SEA

WITH SMOOTH, rhythmic strokes, Tom's assailants paddled steadily out to sea. Neither spoke nor paid the slightest attention to their prisoner.

Despairingly, the young scientist realized that every dip of the blades was carrying him farther from hope of rescue. He tried to free himself from his bonds, but his struggles were useless and nearly tipped over the canoe.

For nearly an hour his abductors paddled seaward. Then, as if by signal, they stopped and allowed the canoes to drift for a while. Again they resumed paddling, then stopped once more.

Tom was puzzled by their actions. When they repeated the procedure a third time, he struggled upward and stared out across the water. Suddenly he realized the reason for their strange actions.

They were looking for a current which would carry him away from Loonaui Island!

In desperation, Tom made another frantic effort to free himself. Bathed in perspiration, he sank back hopelessly in the bottom of the canoe.

"Don't get panicky," Tom said to himself. "You've got to think clearly."

As his mind worked feverishly trying to fathom a way to escape, the natives found the current. The rear paddler plucked a knife from his waist and slashed the rope holding Tom's canoe. Without a second glance at their victim, the men swerved their own craft around and began paddling swiftly back to the island.

A fresh wave of despair swept over Tom as they disappeared in the distance. He wondered why they had not killed him at once. Then he recalled stories Kipu had told of how the natives feared the *akuakus,* or spirits of the dead. According to legend, they were sure to return and haunt a murderer.

For a while Tom lay thinking in the drifting craft. At last he roused himself. *Somehow he must find a way to get free!* If he drifted too far, there would be little hope of rescue, since the island was far from the ocean shipping lanes.

Struggling to an upright position again, he began to examine the canoe thoroughly. Twisting around, he saw the gleam of a shiny object in back of him. Tom's heart gave a leap. It was a broken mirror—perhaps one that his own men had traded to a native!

"What luck!" Tom thought, his heart pounding. By careful maneuvering, he managed to reach the jagged piece of glass with his fingers. Then began a long, nerve-racking job as he sawed, strand by strand, through the ropes that bound his wrists. Darkness had fallen before he finished.

The instant Tom's hands were free, he ripped off the gag and breathed in great gusts of fresh sea air. Then he untied his ankles.

As Tom chafed his legs and wrists, he took stock of the situation. A glance at the stars and the tiny lights on the far-distant island told him that he was still floating steadily away from Loonaui. Without sail or paddle, his plight was growing more hopeless by the second.

"I must get out of this current!" Tom muttered.

Recalling the maneuvers of the native paddlers, he estimated that it would be a two-mile swim to the east, allowing for drift, for him to escape the current.

Hauling in the lead rope, Tom tied it around his waist. The other end was still connected to the bow of the canoe. Then he plunged over the side.

A cool night breeze had sprung up, but the sea felt warm to his skin. Bucking the strong current with slow, easy strokes, Tom swam eastward, dragging the canoe in his wake. It was a strenuous feat, and after half an hour of steady swimming, Tom climbed back into the canoe for a brief rest.

For a good part of the night he continued alternating his grueling swims with periods of rest. Finally he got beyond the current. Then he stretched out in the canoe and fell asleep. When he awoke, the stars had faded and the sun was already well up in the sky.

"Now comes the most dangerous part," Tom thought as it began to grow hotter. "Those villains may send out scouts."

The sky shone like burnished steel, the sun's rays beating down on his naked shoulders with the heat of a blast furnace. To protect himself, Tom submerged alongside the canoe as much as possible. From time to time he flashed signals with the mirror in the direction of the shore to attract attention.

Back on the tiny island, the rocket base was in an uproar. When Tom had failed to return to camp, Bud and Ken Horton had organized a futile search. Now it was morning and still Tom had not appeared.

Bud called a meeting in the palm-thatched cottage which served both as Tom's office and living quarters. Present were all of the Americans at the camp, including Slim Davis, a Swift pilot who had brought in a cargo plane the day before.

"So far we haven't a single lead to help us find Tom," Bud announced glumly.

Horton asked, "What about that trip you made to town yesterday? Did you find out anything about Rhoderman and the Gorilla that might give us a clue?"

Bud ran his fingers through his shock of dark

hair and shook his head in discouragement. "A couple of guys at the harbor saw them come ashore —at least they saw two men who fit the right descriptions. But they figured that the men belonged to our outfit, so they didn't pay much attention. The boat went away again and no one even noticed where it came from."

"Where did they stay after they landed?"

"Search me. There's only one hotel in town and they didn't register there. Or any place else that I could find."

Bob Jeffers, a young mechanic from Swift Enterprises who had qualified for the space crew, spoke up. "What about that guy Pali? Didn't you say he was up to some monkey business awhile back?"

"I've been working on Pali all morning," replied Bud, "but he claims he hasn't seen Tom since he quit work yesterday."

"If you ask me, there's only one thing we *can* do," put in Davis. "We'd better notify the island police pronto!"

At that moment Ken Horton pointed out the window. "Here comes Kipu," he exclaimed. "Looks as though something's up!"

The native burst into the cottage. "I bring news!" he announced breathlessly. "Boat gone from beach. Loonaui man who owns it cannot find it."

Bud jumped up, knocking over his chair in his excitement. "A boat! Why didn't we think of that before? Come on, Ken. Let's go up in the *Skeeter* and take a look!"

The *Skeeter* was a midget helicopter carried on board the *Sky Queen*. Soon it was whirling aloft, carrying Bud and Ken Horton out over the water.

They had circled the island for more than half an hour when Horton blinked his eyes and shouted, "Bud, I see light flashes! I think someone's signaling with a mirror!"

Bud went lower and flew toward the flashes. "It's Tom!" he cried out gleefully.

Moments later, the helicopter was hovering over the canoe and lowering a sling to haul Tom aboard the *Skeeter*.

"Boy, am I glad to see you!" Bud exclaimed, gazing at his exhausted, sunburned friend.

A few gulps of water from a thermos bottle helped to revive Tom. Then he related what had happened.

"That sneaking rat!" Bud growled when he heard how Pali had led Tom into a trap. "Wait till I get my hands on him!" The set of his jaw and the way he hunched his broad shoulders indicated that the young flier meant business.

"Sorry, Bud, but you're not going to touch him," Tom said. "Not right away, anyhow." In answer to Bud's surprised protest, he went on, "Pali's not working alone in this deal. I want to get all of the guys who helped him. There's only one way to do that."

"How?"

"By pretending you didn't find me. I'll stay hidden on that tug, tied up below. If Pali leaves, come and get me and we'll follow him."

After landing, Bud and Ken returned to camp alone, looking troubled. Word quickly spread

Pali lunged toward Bud

around the base that they had found no trace of Tom or the missing canoe.

Pali slipped away from camp at the end of the afternoon. Tom, Bud, Ken, and two policemen followed him into the hills to a grass hut. They crept up to listen.

Inside the hut, the two men who had kidnaped Tom sprang up to greet Pali, eager for news. He replied in a stream of native words, and all three burst into satisfied chuckles.

But their mirth was short-lived. They whirled in surprise as Bud and Ken crowded through the doorway with the two island policemen.

"Okay, Pali. You've had it!" Bud exulted. "These cops just translated your remarks for us. Only you never will collect that money you were talking about, because Tom Swift is still alive!"

As Tom walked in, Pali gave a scream of rage. Grabbing a heavy club, he lunged toward Bud, who quickly flattened Pali with a hard right to the jaw, while the island policemen covered the other two natives.

"Now then, Pali, you'd better talk and talk fast," Tom said. "You'll stand trial for kidnaping, but you can make it easy for yourself by telling what you know."

Pali struggled slowly to his feet, all the fight gone out of him.

"All right," he mumbled. "I'll tell you everything."

CHAPTER 17

WATERFRONT HIDE-OUT

IF PALI told the truth, Tom thought elatedly, he might get to the bottom of the mystery!

The half-breed slumped down on a wooden bench. "I told you I was an engineer. I worked in a factory in the States. But my boss fired me. For revenge, I sabotaged the plant machinery. I was caught and went to prison. After I got out, no one would hire me. Then a man offered me money to come to Loonaui."

"Who was he?" Tom asked.

"His name is Blatka—Stanis Blatka."

"What did this man look like?"

Pali shuddered. "If you ever see his face, you won't forget it. He has a heavy jaw and beetle eyebrows. The man is built like an ape!"

Tom and Bud exchanged glances. The Gorilla!

"What did Blatka want you to do?" Tom asked.

"Stir up the natives and make trouble. He was hoping I might get them to attack your group."

"Well?"

The half-breed shrugged. "The natives wouldn't do it. So Blatka told me to hire canoemen to take you out to sea. You know the rest."

"Why is Blatka out to get me?" Tom prodded when Pali became silent.

The man's eyes showed fear. "I—I'm not sure," he faltered. "But I do know this—he's head of a dangerous group. The rest are the same nationality as Blatka. They're all fanatics—half crazy! As far as I could make out, they're trying to wipe out the top scientists in every country but their own!"

Bud turned to Tom with a startled look. "This must be even bigger than we thought!"

Tom gave a worried and thoughtful nod. "Any idea where we can locate this gang?"

Pali hesitated sullenly, then asked for paper and pencil. Tom handed him a pencil and a slip of paper torn from his notebook. Pali scribbled down an address.

"When I first met Blatka, the gang was using this place in Frisco for a hide-out."

After the police had handcuffed their three prisoners and taken them away, Tom said to Bud, "Come on. Let's get back to camp. I'll radio a report on all this to the FBI. Then you and I are taking off for San Francisco!"

Preparations for the trip were made speedily, and a few hours later the *Sky Queen* was streaking high over the Pacific carrying Tom, Bud, and Ken. The great silvery ship winged in over the Golden Gate Bridge that afternoon. Tom hovered above the airport, cleared with the control tower, and landed gracefully.

As they walked briskly toward the terminal building, a tall man approached the trio and identified himself as Peter T. Stewart, an FBI agent.

After quick introductions, the FBI man said to Tom, "We've surrounded the address you gave us but haven't closed in yet. The chief thought that you might like to be there when we move in!"

"I sure would," Tom replied. "Let's go!"

In the government man's car, they started for the rendezvous. The address proved to be a suite of offices over an empty warehouse in the waterfront district.

"Perfect place for a hide-out," commented Tom, as they parked in front of the building.

"Right," Stewart agreed. "And plenty of room for storing weapons or explosives. We've had men covering the place ever since we got word from you, but so far there's been no sign of life."

After urging the boys to stay close to him, the FBI agent gave his men the signal to close in. There was no answer to their command to open the doors, so they battered them down. Stewart, with Tom, Bud, and Ken at his heels, dashed up the front stairway.

Another group took the back stairs. Two men checked the freight hoist.

The second-floor offices were empty! Stripped shelves, drawers, and files indicated that the occupants had made a hasty getaway.

"I was afraid of this," Stewart commented wryly.

"But who tipped them off?" Bud puzzled.

"I have a hunch that the Gorilla notified his friends by short wave the night we chased him off the island," Tom replied. "He was too smart to take any chances on Pali talking."

Tom thanked the FBI men for their assistance. Peter Stewart promised to get in touch with the Swifts if his men turned up any new leads. Then the boys paid a short visit to Bud's family, now living in San Francisco, after which they took off for Shopton.

The next morning, when Tom arrived at his office, Miss Trent reported that a delegation of government astronomers wanted to talk with Tom about his space station observatory as soon as possible. The young inventor suggested that Miss Trent arrange for a meeting the following afternoon at three o'clock.

Promptly at three the next day the group of scientists arrived at the Swifts' office. Dr. Amos Harlow, head of the delegation, was a pleasant man with twinkling eyes and bushy white hair.

After outlining his plans, Tom showed them the model of his proposed outpost in space. "These two sections," he said, pointing, "will be assigned to astronomical work. Of the others, two will be used for making solar batteries, three for commercial broadcasting, one for government broadcasting, one for medical purposes, one as my private lab, one for sleeping quarters, and one for dining and recreation."

"A brilliant job of design!" commented Dr. Harlow. "Now let us show you our plans for the space telescope."

He unrolled a sheaf of drawings. "As you can see, the optical elements will be held together by a mere spiderwork of wires. The heavy mirrors will be weightless out there in space, so this is all we'll need to brace them rigidly."

Compared to the giant telescopes used on the earth, the space telescope would be small. But Dr. Harlow explained that it would give a much clearer, sharper picture of the heavens because there would be none of the earth's atmosphere to blur out the view.

"Think how the skies will open to us!" the white-haired astronomer said enthusiastically. "We'll be able to study the dust clouds in the Milky Way, and those strange exploding stars called supernovae. With luck, we'll learn about life on Mars—perhaps even solve the riddle of how the universe was formed!"

Tom's pulse throbbed with excitement. He could hardly wait to complete his outpost! After the details of mounting the telescope had been worked out, the elated astronomers arose to say good-by.

"We'll meet you on Loonaui," was their parting remark.

After their departure, Tom drove to the main laboratory. The engineers assigned to the air-conditioning setup in the space station had asked to see him.

Jack Grady, the chief engineer, greeted him with a pleased grin. "It looks as if we have the oxygen supply problem licked, Tom. Thanks to your dad!"

"By using those chlorella algae?" Tom asked, referring to the tiny green water plants.

"Right. We've just finished running tests on the stuff. In strong sunlight, five tankfuls of those plants will absorb carbon dioxide and give off enough oxygen for a crew of fifty men!"

"Fine. How big are the tanks?"

"Five feet square and filled to a depth of one inch," replied Grady. "They're in a greenhouse on the roof."

"How about the moisture problem?"

"We're working on that." Grady pointed through a glass window to several men in a sealed test chamber that was filled with a foglike haze. "According to our estimates, a man needs about two quarts of water a day. Half of it he gives off to the atmosphere by breathing and evaporation. That much we can recover, purify, and use over again."

"The rest we'll have to bring up, I suppose," said Tom.

"Right. About one quart per man."

Tom rubbed his chin thoughtfully. "Well, we can save the weight of containers by bringing it up frozen into cakes of ice."

Grady snapped his fingers. "Tom, that's an idea! As the ice melts in the space station, it'll take part of the load off the air-conditioning system, too!"

Tom slapped Grady on the back and said with a grin, "Well, that's my quota of help for the day!"

On the way back to his office Tom stopped off at the Zero-G chamber. Bud stood at the controls. Inside the chamber, a man in one of the fishlike test suits was wallowing and flopping wildly about in mid-air as he tried to adjust his muscles to his helpless condition.

"That's Chow in there!" Bud exclaimed.

Tom chuckled. "I might have known!"

The two boys were weak with laughter by the time Chow emerged. His bowlegs wobbled weakly as he removed his metal cap.

"That blamed setup is worse'n the meanest bronc I ever rid!" the chef announced mournfully. "I'm still wonderin' how I'm goin' to do any cookin' up there in the middle o' nowhere!"

"You won't have much cooking to do," Tom informed him. "The food will be shipped up precooked and frozen. All you'll need to do will be heat it in an electronic oven."

Chow groaned. "Tom, that's an insult to any self-respectin' range cook!"

Then the old Westerner suddenly changed the subject. "Brand my ceilin' chuck wagon, I plumb forgot to show you a letter I got, Tom! It's enough to drive a cowhand loco!"

CHAPTER 18

A DEADLY TRICK

"WHAT LETTER?" Tom asked, puzzled by the cook's worried expression.

"Jest come in the mail this mornin'. Reckon you better take a look at it. The envelope has a San Antonio postmark."

A small locker room had been partitioned off near the Zero-G chamber for trainees to change into their test suits. Chow led the way there. A gaudy orange-and-green Western shirt was hanging on a hook. He pulled a lettter from the breast pocket.

The letter had been written in a rough, sprawling hand. It read:

Dear Chow:
 I heard you was working for the Swift outfit, so I figgered it was my duty to write and warn you.

Yesterday my boss was gabbing with an Army rocket man and, believe me, I heard an earful about Tom Swift. Chow, that boy has gone plumb loco, because only a crazy man would try that space station thing he is working on!

The Army man said the way Tom Swift was making his rockets, they would blow up before they ever got off the ground. My boss said he heard Washington was going to investigate, and he hoped they would stop Tom Swift before anyone got killed.

Well, partner, if you're smart, you'll haul your chuck wagon away from there pronto and tell all your friends to do likewise. Take my advice and come back to Texas before you get mixed up in a nasty investigation or else get blown sky-high!

Your old pal,

Ben

Tom was shocked by the letter. "Who's this Ben?"

Chow scratched his bald head. "That's the funny part o' the whole business. I've met half a dozen hombres named Ben, but I don't know which one wrote this!" After a second's pause, he added, "Course I'm stickin' with your shindig, no matter who wrote the letter. Even if you was flyin' clear up to the moon! But I sure would like to know what's back o' this here warning!"

Tom frowned. "Chow, the person who wrote it **is** certainly trying to make trouble."

"Or else," said Bud, "he's nutty as a fruitcake!"

Chow turned the letter over to Tom, who promptly took it to the security office. Ames and Radnor read it with angry interest. Both sized it up the same way—a "war-of-nerves" move aimed to wreck Tom's project.

"Sounds to me like something that fellow Rhoderman might do." Ames frowned. "I'll check immediately to see if any similar letters have been received by other men at the plant."

Tom decided to phone the president of the Quik Battery Corporation at once for information on Rhoderman. A few moments later York came on the line.

"Well, what do you want, Swift?" he growled.

"I'm calling to inquire about one of your salesmen —a fellow named Eli Rhoderman," Tom said.

"What about him?"

"Have you heard from him recently?"

York hesitated. "Well, no. Not for a few weeks."

"Is he still working for you?"

"Of course he's working for me!" York snapped. Even over the telephone, Tom could imagine the man's bullfrog eyes bulging out and his face getting redder with irritation. "Rhoderman's been on a long sales trip, that's all. We don't keep our men on a leash. We give 'em plenty of leeway!"

"Enough to get mixed up in subversion and sabotage?"

York gasped. "What are you talking about, Swift?" he challenged with angry bluster.

Tom gave him a brief fill-in on Rhoderman's recent activities, including his furtive visit to Loonaui, and also mentioned his tie-up with the Gorilla.

"Poppycock!" York exploded. "Rhoderman's one of our top salesmen. If you expect me to believe your crazy suspicions, you've got another think coming!"

"Sorry I wasted your time," replied Tom dryly.

"Well, just so the price of this call won't be wasted, let me give *you* a tip," York gloated. "Watch the papers for a big announcement!" He slammed down the receiver, and Tom hung up thoughtfully, wondering what York meant.

A few days later Tom was seated at the breakfast table, eating griddlecakes and bacon, when Sandy raced into the dining room with a copy of the morning paper. "Tom, look!" she cried in dismay, thrusting the front page under her brother's eyes. Bold black headlines proclaimed:

NEW INVENTION WILL HARNESS SUN'S ENERGY

Tom scanned the story quickly. It announced that the Quik Battery Corporation had developed a solar battery that would revolutionize industry. York was quoted in glowing terms in praise of the many future uses for the battery. The story also stated that the batteries were energized in space but gave no further details.

Tom handed the paper to his father, who read the news release with a troubled frown. "Those balloons you saw must be the answer," Mr. Swift remarked when he had finished. "Matter of fact, I've heard reports that a whole series of such balloons has been sighted lately."

At that moment Phyl Newton arrived. Her eyes were flashing fire. She had read the item and an editorial as well.

"It's disgraceful!" she exclaimed, and read the editorial aloud.

"Local citizens will regret that the Quik Battery Corporation has succeeded in making a solar battery before our own Swift Enterprises. Shopton has always looked forward to the Swifts being first in their field with new scientific achievements. But in this case, John York and his staff have snatched the laurels from our famous father-and-son team."

"That's an insult!" Mrs. Swift exclaimed.

"My dad was furious when he read this," Phyl reported. "He says the *Bulletin* had no right to make such sarcastic comments!"

Mr. Swift remained strangely silent.

Tom shrugged his shoulders as he pushed back his chair from the table and said, "It's a free country. If York's battery is all he claims, more power to him."

But inwardly Tom felt sick. As he drove to Enterprises, he reflected on whether this revelation might affect his outpost-in-space project. If York's battery captured the market, it might not pay the Swifts to manufacture theirs 22,300 miles above the earth. A great deal of the money that his father's company had invested in the project would be wasted!

As soon as he reached his office, Tom called a friend who ran an electrical engineering firm in Philadelphia. He told him what had happened. "See if you can obtain one of Quik's solar batteries, Jerry, so we can run some tests on it. I doubt if York would sell me one direct."

"Sure thing, Tom!"

To help forget his worries, the young inventor buried himself in work. One good thing, Tom mused, as he bent over his drawing board, was that everything else was going along well on his project. He and the other Enterprises engineers were conquering the various problems in connection with the space station.

Late that afternoon a phone call came from Washington. The caller was Dr. Madden, of the Public Health Service, one of the government medical men cooperating in the Swifts' project.

"Your idea of using an oxygen-helium mixture to breathe looks good, Tom!" he reported. "Our tests show that it'll cut down the danger of your crew suffering from bends in case of an air leak."

Tom was jubilant as he hung up. Helium weighed less than the nitrogen in ordinary air. So it would also cut down on the weight of the breathing mixture needed to fill the station.

Tom hurried to the main laboratory, eager to carry out a few more tests along the same lines. To his surprise, he found that his empty tank of oxygen had been replaced by a new one bearing the label of the Aer-Cel Company. Picking up the phone, Tom dialed the supply department.

"What happened to our own tanks of oxygen, Barney?" he asked. "I notice this new cylinder is from the Aer-Cel Company."

"That's one they gave us free," explained the warehouse man. "Seems they've designed a new regulator for their tanks and they'd like you to try it out. I figured you wouldn't mind."

"Not a bit. I just wondered, that's all."

Tom hung up and examined the device which Barney had referred to. It was wired to the cap nut on the tank, and included a pressure gauge, stopcock, and the necessary threaded fittings for attachment.

Tom unwired the gadget and screwed it into place on the tank. Then he adjusted the tank valve to a suitable pressure and opened the stopcock, to draw off a small amount of oxygen.

The young inventor was puzzled. The device seemed to work in the usual way. Yet there was something queer about the design.

Tom tried to shut off the flow, but the stopcock would not turn. He tried the tank valve. This, too, refused to budge!

Suddenly Tom felt ill. A strange paralysis seemed

to be numbing his arms and legs. In a flash, he realized that he had been duped by a trick. Instead of oxygen, there was a deadly gas in the tank!

Tom knew that he must get out of the room before he was overcome. But, as he tried to go forward, he staggered—it seemed as though his legs just wouldn't move!

CHAPTER 19

ORBIT 22,300

GROGGY from the deadly gas, Tom lurched toward the door of his laboratory. With one hand, he pulled out his handkerchief and held it to his nose. But his legs dragged as though weighted down with lead.

"I'll never make it!" he thought.

Then Tom remembered the wall switch for the exhaust fans. It was just a few steps away. If he could only reach it!

He stumbled forward. One hand groped up and dragged down the lever. The exhaust blowers whirred into life.

Tom felt a surge of air. But the gas from the tank was filling the room. His head was splitting. Swaying blindly, he lurched on . . . two steps . . . three steps . . . one more now and he could reach the door!

It seemed like a lifetime before his hand closed on the knob. With a superhuman effort, Tom opened the door and staggered into the hallway. He was just in time—everything was blacking out. As the heavy steel door swung shut behind him, Tom slumped to the floor!

Down the corridor a workman raised a shout of alarm. Men came running from all directions. Mr. Swift was the first to reach his son's side.

"Tom! What happened?" his father cried, cradling the youth's head with one arm.

The young inventor's lips moved weakly. He mumbled a single word, "Gas . . ."

"Don't go into that lab!" Mr. Swift shouted as someone opened the door to peer inside.

The atmosphere of the air-conditioned building soon revived Tom. Gradually the color returned to his cheeks and his eyes opened.

"Don't try to talk yet, son."

When Tom felt completely revived, he accompanied his father into the laboratory. By this time, the blowers had cleared the room of gas and the air was safe to breathe.

Mr. Swift sniffed the tank cautiously. A faint trace of gas was still evident. He caught some in a burette and tried several chemicals on it. When he was through, he looked at Tom.

"Know what that stuff was?" he asked grimly.

"Some type of nerve gas, I imagine."

"Fluorophosphonate ester. Son, if you hadn't

made it to the door in time, you'd be dead by now!"

Tom shuddered. "I wonder if the Aer-Cel Company really did send me that tank?"

"We'll find out right now!"

Mr. Swift picked up the phone and asked the operator to get the president of the Aer-Cel Company. Tom listened to the conversation, then flashed a questioning look as his father hung up.

"He knows nothing about it—says they never sent over any tank of oxygen," Mr. Swift reported.

"In other words, somebody pulled a fast one!"

Father and son stared at each other, sharing the same sobering thought. *Evidently Tom's enemies were still at work and would stop at nothing!*

"Tom," said Mr. Swift with determination, "you're to have protection at all times from now on."

One afternoon Bud found Chow parked outside the laboratory door as a specially appointed guard. Inside, Tom was hard at work with a slide rule. His desk was littered with papers, each one covered with figures and equations. From time to time the young scientist paused to feed a new problem into a small electronic computer.

"What gives, chum?" Bud asked.

Tom grinned and ran his fingers through his blond crew cut. "Just working out the ascent track for the rockets."

"What a headache!"

"We want to circle the earth in an orbit 22,300

miles up. But the trick is to make our rockets hit the orbit at just the right spot."

"Where'll that be?"

"Directly above Ecuador in South America," replied Tom. "The broadcasters figure that will be the best spot for sending and receiving signals."

"Got the course all figured out?"

"Just about. We'll go straight up for ten miles, then veer east. By the time we're a thousand miles up, we'll be zooming along at 21,000 an hour."

Bud gave an awed whistle as Tom continued, "At that point, we'll cut the engines and coast the rest of the way. We'll travel in an elliptical track around the earth till we reach our final altitude. Then, one more spurt of power to get us started in our orbit, and we're in business! But the only way to make sure we've got the right path—and a safe one—is to try it."

"You mean, make a preliminary flight before you send up the space station rockets?"

Tom nodded. "I'm looking for a passenger. Want to apply?"

"You couldn't leave me behind, you old space eagle."

"Thanks, Bud." Tom's expression showed his appreciation of his friend's loyalty. "We'll take the *Star Spear*."

The *Star Spear* was the famous rocket ship in which the boys had won an international prize for making the first free orbital flight around the earth.

Tom said that he had improved the fuel kicker in it, and they now could go to far greater heights.

Bud wandered over to the window. "Good weather tomorrow. Let's get started first thing in the morning."

Before Tom could reply, Miss Trent called in a message for Tom. "A crate just arrived from your friend in Philadelphia," she said. "It contains one of those new solar batteries made by the Quik Corporation."

"Arrange to have it brought to my laboratory at once," Tom said excitedly.

CHAPTER 20

A PRISONER TALKS

TOM PACED up and down impatiently in his laboratory until the crate arrived. Then he and Bud quickly ripped off the slats with chisels.

"So that's York's latest baby," Bud remarked, as he lifted the shiny black battery to Tom's workbench.

He watched intently while his friend hooked it up to a voltmeter, then closed a switch on the control board. The needle swung far around the dial.

Bud gasped. "Hey, that's as powerful as your battery!"

Tom nodded with a worried frown. "Right. And what's worse, York's beaten us to the punch by putting it on the market. By the time we bring out our model, the Quik outfit may have things all sewed up!"

The young inventor set up a test chamber for

aging the device, similar to the one that he had made for testing his own battery in the Fearing Island laboratory. While he was hooking the Quik battery to it, Radnor and Ames came to report that they were about to take off for San Francisco to do some work for the FBI in tracking down Blatka and his cohorts. Tom wished them better luck than he was having at the moment.

As he headed home that evening, Tom was dejected. So far, York's battery looked much better than he had expected. Then he shook off the glum mood.

"Tomorrow's results will tell the story. Why worry now?"

Early the next morning Tom gulped down a hasty breakfast and drove to his laboratory. With eager fingers, he ripped off the electric leads and pulled the battery out of the test chamber. Then he hooked it up again to the voltmeter on his control board. The needle flickered weakly. The battery was almost dead!

Tom gave a whoop of relief. It was clear that York's engineers had failed to conquer the problem of how to keep their battery from discharging too fast. Tom's, on the other hand, had stood up under heavy testing. It would hold its charge for years!

To make sure of his findings, Tom proceeded to disassemble the Quik battery and analyze every part of it. He grew so interested that he worked on through lunchtime without stopping to eat. The tests showed that some parts of York's product were made of new materials which his scientists had invented.

"But their desensitizer is almost worthless," Tom concluded.

He was startled by a feminine voice, asking, "Doesn't your phone work, brother?"

He looked up in surprise to see Sandy and Phyl grinning at him from the doorway.

"We've been trying to call you ever since one o'clock," Phyl said with a mock frown.

Tom's eyes twinkled. "To tell you the truth, I turned off the phone this morning so I wouldn't be interrupted. I forgot to switch it on again."

"Talk about absent-minded geniuses!" Phyl teased.

"Okay, so I'm a blockhead," Tom retorted with a chuckle. As he wiped his hands with a rag, the two pretty girls perched themselves on one of the laboratory benches. "And now," said Tom, "own up. You didn't come just to watch me work."

"I'd like permission to take up the heliplane," Sandy announced.

"Sure, go ahead. Pleasure or business?"

"Business. I've found a prospective customer." Sandy's eyes sparkled with mischief. "He's very handsome, too."

"Bud won't like that," warned Tom jokingly.

"Huh!" Sandy made a wry face. "If Phyl and I waited for you and Bud to take us out, we'd be twiddling our thumbs most of the time!"

Tom grinned. "You've got us there, Sis. But let's fix that right now. What about a double date this evening? Dinner, movies, and dancing afterward."

The girls agreed, then asked what was keeping Tom so busy. They were overjoyed to hear that York had not outwitted the young inventor after all.

"And my dad will be happy to hear it," Phyl said.

That evening, Bud called for Phyl, then drove to the Swift home. The girls, dressed in gay dancing frocks, looked at the boys and smiled. "Who are these strangers, Phyl?" teased Sandy. "White shirts, ties, suits—why, I don't recognize them!"

As the four were about to leave, Tom saw the red light flash on their home videophone. He hurried over to flick on the set. Ted Elheimer, the West Coast telecaster, came on the screen from San Francisco.

"Tom! Radnor and Ames just phoned!" he reported. "They've nabbed a man they believe is Rhoderman. If he can be definitely identified, they hope he'll talk. They want you to fly out here immediately."

"Tell 'em I'll be there in a couple of hours!" Tom said, as Sandy and Phyl groaned with disappointment.

Tom flipped off the videophone and grinned. "Why spoil the fun? Let's all fly out there! We'll stop at your house, Phyl, so that you can tell your parents and change your clothes."

After leaving the Newton house, they picked up Ken Horton to identify Rhoderman, then drove to the Enterprises airfield.

Soon the *Sky Queen* was roaring westward at twelve hundred miles an hour. California skies were clear for the landing. The young people hurried to the telecasting studio where Radnor and Ames were holding their prisoner. He had a livid bruise below one eye and a bandage taped across his temple which Ames said he had when picked up.

"That's Rhoderman, all right," Ken said. "He's the man I saw on the beach in Florida."

Realizing that the situation was hopeless, the salesman began to talk. He admitted leaving the note in the bottle and sending the warning flash to Tom over the videophone, as well as the message to Kane about Horton being a foreign agent. He had also written the fake letter to Chow.

"What were you doing on Loonaui?" Tom asked. "We saw you with Blatka, so you might as well tell the whole truth."

Rhoderman shrugged sullenly. "You can probably guess, so why ask? I was sent to help stir up the natives and ruin your plans for a rocket base." But Rhoderman denied knowing anything about Tom's kidnapers or of the other attacks on the two boys.

"Now let's hear *why* you did all this," Ames hammered away at him.

"And don't expect us to believe that it was all for the dear old Quik Battery Corporation!" Bud scoffed.

Rhoderman explained that he had been bribed by Blatka to find out all he could about the Swifts. He had heard of Tom's solar battery and the space station project through a pal named Herkim. This man had wormed his way into a job at the Enterprises plant. Later, after Herkim had been fired for seemingly loafing on the job, Rhoderman had been paid to help wreck Tom's plans.

Ames kept on firing questions at the salesman. "Where can we find Blatka?" he demanded.

"I've told you everything!" Rhoderman pleaded. "I never did know what Blatka was up to, and I never cared, as long as he kept shelling out money."

"I'm asking you where we can find him!" repeated Ames with bulldog grimness.

"I tell you I don't know! Last time I saw him, he got sore because I wanted no part of his plans for knocking off Swift. I figured that he was going too far. So he beat me up and I haven't seen him since!"

To prove his story, Rhoderman pointed to his bruised face. Tom and Ames exchanged glances. It looked as though the salesman was telling the truth.

"Now I've even lost my job," Rhoderman whined. "York found out what I was up to and fired me!"

Tom felt that they had learned all they could, and told Ames to turn Rhoderman over to the FBI.

The next morning, before Bud was awake, Tom

returned to the studio and made a short-wave call to Loonaui Island. When he joined Bud and the girls for breakfast at the Barclay home, he made a surprise announcement:

"What say we fly right on to Loonaui? The *Star Spear* is out there, and it's all set for Bud and me to make our rocket test for the flight track. So why wait?"

CHAPTER 21

BLAST-OFF!

THE PROPOSAL of a flight to Loonaui thrilled
Phyl and Sandy. "And let's ask Mother and Dad,
too," Tom's sister suggested. "I'm sure that they'd
like to see you and Bud off on your rocket hop."

"Good idea, Sis! I'll call Shopton."

Mr. Swift, who received the call in his office,
promised that he and his wife would start for the
Pacific that day.

By noontime the *Sky Queen* was winging over the
sea. Ken Horton, Ames, and Radnor were aboard.
Several hours later they swooped in low over the
coral reefs and settled down on the Loonaui airfield.

The girls were enthralled by the beautiful, lush
island. "Is this ever dreamy!" Sandy exclaimed.

She and Phyl embarked at once on a tour of the
island. Tom and the others plunged into work.
Ames and Radnor took on the job of organizing an

airtight security system for Loonaui. The boys, with
a crew, began to assemble the *Star Spear*, which had
been shipped out in sections by cargo plane.

Work continued in shifts throughout the night.
By the next afternoon the four-stage, red-finned
rocket stood poised on its concrete launching platform inside a light metal scaffolding.

"It won't be long now!" Tom remarked to Bud.

As the boys stopped in the blockhouse to look over
the launching controls and radar-tracking equipment, George Dilling paused in his work. "Electronic circuits all checked, Tom!"

"Good!"

Tom double-checked every detail of the rocket inside and out. In the pilot's cabin in the nose, Tom
took a final look at the flight plan, punched out on
plastic tape. Then he fed the tape into the electric
brain which would steer the ship through space.

"We're practically on our way!" Bud exclaimed.

Early that evening Mr. and Mrs. Swift landed on
Loonaui. Tom told them the take-off would be the
next day.

As darkness fell on the island, the girls staged a
gay beach party as a farewell. By the light of blazing
bonfires, a native feast was served, accompanied by
music.

Mrs. Swift tried hard to enjoy the party, but Tom
could see that her heart was not in it. "Cheer up,
Mother," he comforted her. "Bud and I are old
hands at rocket flight."

Mrs. Swift smiled and blinked back tears. "I never got used to your father's adventures, and I guess I'll never get used to yours, Tom." Then she recalled her blushing girlhood days when she had made her first airplane flight with Tom Sr. Everyone laughed as she described the terror-filled five-minute trip.

Before going to bed, Tom listened to a report from Harlan Ames. "Armed guards will patrol the launching area constantly," he said. "And our boys up there in the sky will prevent any air attack." The security chief pointed to a ring of aircraft circling the island in the star-studded darkness.

"Thanks, Harlan! I guess the rest of us can sleep peacefully."

Tom and Bud chatted quietly in their bunks. Each was thoughtful as he listened to the whisper of the trade winds and soft splashing of the breakers. Finally, they fell asleep.

The next thing the boys knew, they were awakened by a weird whistling shriek. They leaped up in alarm and dashed outside.

Giant searchlights swept the sky. They locked suddenly on a blurred object skimming in from the sea.

"It's a bomb!" yelled Bud.

The boys froze with suspense. The missile was arrowing straight toward the rocket base!

"It's going to miss!" Tom shouted, as the missile passed over the island and plowed into the waters beyond with a thunderous roar.

The boys dressed frantically and sped off in a jeep

to join Harlan Ames. Planes were streaking out to sea.

"The radar crew tracked the course of the bomb," Ames reported. "It must have been fired from a ship."

But when the search planes found no sign of a vessel, Tom concluded that the missile had been launched from a low-flying plane.

Mrs. Swift was terrified. "Tom, your enemies are so determined. Don't you think that it would be wise to give up your space trip?"

Tom smiled. "Judging from tonight, I'll be safer up in the air than I will be down here!"

As dawn broke, trucks rumbled back and forth between the fuel-storage tanks and the launching area, piping alcohol and liquid oxygen into the *Star Spear*. Mechanics swarmed about the rocket, checking lines, valves, and pumps.

Soon it was time for blast-off. Tom hugged his mother fondly, whispering words of reassurance, then shook hands with his dad.

"Good luck, son," said Mr. Swift tensely.

After farewell kisses from Sandy and Phyl, the boys rode up to the nose section of the rocket. The conveyor was then withdrawn and the opening in each stage sealed off.

"Radar report!" Tom radioed to the blockhouse.

Gleaming scanner dishes began sweeping the sky, like the huge antennae of some fantastic insect.

"All clear!" George Dilling called back.

In the pilot's cabin Tom set the flight tape in action. Time clocks began ticking in the blockhouse. The boys strapped themselves to their couches.

Outside, the onlookers waited tensely. A voice boomed over the loud-speaker:

"X minus five! Please clear the launching area!"

The minutes ticked away . . . *"minus three, minus two, minus one!"*

The ground shook with a blast of thunder! A billowing cloud of smoke and flame burst over the area as the *Star Spear* rose from its launching pad. Slowly at first, then with ever-increasing speed, the rocket shot upward into the blue.

The shock of take-off had flattened the boys against their couches with paralyzing force. But the acceleration pressure eased off somewhat as Tom's anti-G neutralator began to take effect. Already they could feel a sideward pull as the rocket began veering eastward.

Radio signals came through at regular intervals. "Check time!" called Dilling's voice.

"One-two-five seconds!" Tom reported.

"Check speed!"

"Three-eight-four-zero miles per hour!"

A red light flashed on the control panel, and a warning buzzer sounded. Seconds later, the ship quivered as the electronic timer gun fired to cut loose the first stage.

A steel mesh parachute streamed out behind the dropped-off rocket section. Gradually it drifted off on its downward plunge to the ocean far below. Salvage ships would bring it back to Loonaui.

Meanwhile, the *Star Spear* continued its climb into space. Soon the second stage was jettisoned. As the boys waited, Tom watched the gauges and responded to Dilling's radio signals. Finally the red light and buzzer signaled third-stage cutoff.

"This is it!" murmured Tom.

They were now a thousand miles above the Pacific and climbing eastward at the terrifying speed of 21,-000 miles per hour!

As the release gun kicked loose the third stage, the red light flashed off. The thunder of the rocket motors was replaced by an awesome silence. From here on, the rocket would coast up to its orbit.

Now that the ship was no longer accelerating, the G-pressure melted away. Bud swung his couch into sitting position and released his safety belt.

"Boy, do I feel—!" Bud broke off with a gasp as he found himself floating to the cabin roof. With one hand he pushed himself down again. "Good thing I had some lessons in your Zero-G chamber, Tom."

Weightless, Bud cavorted around the cabin like a swimmer in space, then settled down to stare out the porthole. "Man, look at that view!" he exclaimed.

The earth was now far below, with the islands and continents clearly defined.

"May as well relax a bit. It'll be more than four hours before we use the motors again," Tom remarked. "Turn on the oscilloscope and let's see if our space friends have any messages for us."

Bud did so and instantly mathematical symbols began to form on the screen.

"Bud!" Tom exclaimed. "They're warning us of danger!"

"What kind of danger?"

"I don't know. They don't explain."

Tom pressed a button and the metal lid covering the transparent pilot's canopy drew back. Outside, the weird blackness of space shone with myriads of stars. The boys could see no cause for alarm.

Bud flicked on the radar set and began pulsing out radar waves in all directions. But no echoes appeared on the screen from objects in close range.

Tom was puzzled. "Sure wish I knew what they were talking about!"

"Maybe some enemy's chasing us," Bud suggested.

"You mean Blatka?"

The copilot gulped. "Maybe even something from another planet!"

As the minutes went by, with the *Star Spear* now traveling at 4,000 miles an hour, the warning signals continued. But the boys were unable to locate the danger.

Tom switched on his high orbital radio altimeter. The *Star Spear* was more than 21,700 miles up. And a fix with the stellar sextant showed that the ship was almost over Ecuador, the ideal location.

"Stand by for the adaptation maneuver!" Tom told Bud. "We've almost reached our orbit!"

Moments later, the steering motors fired to tilt the ship into proper orbital aim. Then the main rocket motors roared into life. The next second, a blip appeared in the center of the radar screen.

At the same moment, Bud yelled, "There's the danger!"

Tom looked outside. Dead ahead in their orbit and speeding toward them was an unrecorded asteroid or moonlet! Tom had less than half a minute to get out of its path.

Horrified, he ripped out the flight tape and grabbed the steering control to alter course. But something jammed. Frantically, he tugged and pulled. Still the controls would not budge!

The *Star Spear* hurtled toward a head-on collision!

CHAPTER 22

THE MYSTERIOUS WHEEL

WITH INSTANT DEATH only seconds away, Bud sprang to Tom's aid. Together, they wrenched at the controls. But the steering mechanism remained frozen!

The boys stared at each other, white-faced with fear. The moonlet was growing bigger by the moment as the *Star Spear* raced toward it!

Tom gritted his teeth. "The kicker! It's our only chance!"

This device was the heart of the *Star Spear's* power plant. By absorbing the sun's radiation, it changed the liquid oxygen into an exceedingly potent fuel.

"It's hopeless!" Bud gasped. "We're still building up to orbital speed! A fresh burst now won't lift us off our course—it'll only slam us into a collision that much faster!"

"It may free the steering motors!" Tom shouted. "Get back on your couch!"

With one hand he yanked the kicker lever wide open. The rocket zoomed ahead with a violent shudder. In the same instant, Tom gave a do-or-die yank on the steering controls. *This time they responded!*

As the steering jets swung free, the *Star Spear* blasted upward. So near was the moment of collision that the ship almost grazed the hurtling moonlet. It whizzed by at ten miles per second.

The terrific ascent left the boys gasping for breath. Pinned against his couch, Tom could barely manipulate the throttle. But he lowered the rocket, and with a final tilt of the steering jets, directed the ship into its orbital direction.

"Good night!" Bud cried. "If you stay in this path, we'll crash that moonlet when it comes back."

Tom grinned, though he sagged weakly back against his back rest. "Bud, I have a confession to make. I fouled up the flight tape and overshot our intended orbit by a hundred miles. Now we're where we belong!"

Bud groaned. "You old star chaser. Listen! After this, take those free rides alone. I don't like the traffic!"

Tom sat up, grabbed a telescope, and tracked it on the moonlet. The asteroid was rocky and barren—a tiny lost world circling forever as a captive of Mother Earth. He reported this to the copilot.

"Suppose there's any life on it?" Bud asked.

"Not likely, Bud, but someday let's land and find out." Then, after a pause, he said, "I think I'll boost our speed to 14,000 miles an hour."

This speed would enable the *Star Spear* to race around the globe twice as fast as the earth was turning. Thus, instead of remaining above Ecuador, they could check the entire orbit in twenty-four hours.

But it posed a new problem. At such a speed, the earth would lose still more of its grip. The ship would race farther into outer space. To offset this, Tom would have to adjust his steering jets and give the rocket a downward thrust to keep it in the orbit.

Tom pulled out pencil and paper and did some quick calculating. Then he twirled a knob on the flight panel and reset the steering motor controls.

With both boys strapped in place for the im-

Suddenly the strange object veered sharply

minent acceleration, Tom pressed the starter and opened the kicker. The needle climbed to 10,000 miles per hour, 12,000, 13,500 . . . At the right moment, Tom's hand shoved the kicker shut.

"Whew!" Bud breathed. "Genius boy, that gadget of yours is worth its weight in gold!"

As the hours crept by, the earth turned slowly beneath them. North and South America swung past . . . the Atlantic unrolled . . . Europe and Africa came into full view.

Tom and Bud took turns snatching an hour or two of sleep. While one rested, the other kept a visual lookout and watched the radar screen, with occasional glances at the orbital flight indicator.

"I guess that asteroid's the only hazard around here," yawned Bud as they raced into the final lap of their journey. "Our orbit's all clear."

Tom nodded. "I believe a point directly above Loonaui will be the best spot for our space station."

Bud was staring out the canopy. "Mighty con-

and headed straight for the Star Spear

venient having those space friends of yours to watch out for our safety. Wonder where they are now?"

"On their Martian satellite probably."

"I'm not so sure," Bud mused. "They may be—" He broke off and gripped Tom's arm. "Look!"

In the black void of space a spot of light was arcing across the sky. Tom gasped in astonishment.

"What is it?" Bud puzzled. "A shooting star?"

"Can't be—not up here! Shooting stars are just meteors that burn up in the earth's atmosphere."

"Then what in the name of astronautics is it?"

Tom tried to control his excitement. "Bud, it may be a spaceship!"

Suddenly the speeding light veered sharply. It headed straight for the *Star Spear!*

Tom was in a quandary. Could this be his space friends trying to make contact? Or was it a dangerous attacker from outer space?

Closer and closer came the strange object. Tom gunned the steering jets to maneuver the *Star Spear* out of the way. The object, a mammoth silver wheel whirling at terrific rate, shot past.

"Roarin' rockets!" exclaimed Bud. "That looked like your space-wheel design."

"And I'll bet our space friends are on board!" said Tom. "Let's see if we can't contact them."

Warming up the transmitter, he began beaming out signals which he modulated into the wave form of the space symbols. But no reply appeared on the scope.

Suddenly Bud gave a cry of alarm and pointed. "Hey, skipper, the fuel gauge is almost at the empty mark. We'd better get back to earth pronto!"

With a start, Tom realized their full peril. Would they have enough fuel for their landing maneuver? If not, they might be marooned in space, or be unable to control their descent through the earth's atmosphere without danger of burning up!

CHAPTER 23

UNSEEN RAIDERS

"BEGINNING descent maneuver!" Tom radioed back to Loonaui.

He dialed reverse on the flight-position indicator, then switched on the gyros. Instantly the *Star Spear* began to pivot around in a back flip while still hurtling through space on its orbital flight.

"Hit the couch, Bud, and strap your seat belt!"

Tom watched the position indicator like a hawk. The instant the ship reached a tail-forward position, he switched off the gyros and yanked open the kicker.

The rocket motors roared into life with a blast dead ahead. The *Star Spear* shuddered from the terrific braking effect. As the ship slowed abruptly, it peeled off from its orbit and plunged earthward in a cometlike dive. Almost in the same instant, the rocket motors coughed and died.

Bud turned a worried face to his pal. "Think we killed enough speed, skipper? That rocket fuel gave out a bit too soon."

Tom kept his eyes on the speed gauge. "We can make it, if we don't heat up too much. Have to brake pretty hard, once we hit the atmosphere."

Plunging downward at blinding speed, the *Star Spear* swung halfway around the earth in a few hours. As its wings bit into the first thin layers of air, Tom slammed the control stick forward. The boys felt the queer sensation of returning gravity. It was like shooting up in an express elevator!

"What's the skin temperature?" asked Bud.

"Thirteen hundred degrees Fahrenheit!"

Glowing like a red meteor from the heat of air friction, the *Star Spear* hurtled around the night side of the earth. Gradually, Tom plowed deeper into the atmosphere. The ship was now functioning like an airplane in a supersonic glide. Its red glow died away as their tremendous speed decreased in the drag imposed by the heavier air.

Day was dawning over Russia and the bleak steppes of Asia. Tom radioed to Dilling:

"Now approaching the Pacific!"

Slowly the speed indicator flickered downward: . . . 1,050 . . . 1,000 . . . 950 . . .

As they neared Loonaui, jet planes swarmed out to guide them back to the base. Moments later, the *Star Spear* settled safely down on the island runway.

Bud unsealed the escape hatch. With happy grins

the boys emerged from their rocket to a din of shouts and cheers.

Tom's mother smiled through tears of relief as her son greeted her with an affectionate hug and kiss. Mr. Swift welcomed the boys with handclasps and congratulations. Then it was the girls' turn.

"Bring us back any stardust?" Sandy laughed.

"Just a moonbeam apiece," Bud quipped.

"And a kiss for good measure," added Tom, with a grin at Phyl, as the boys proceeded to suit the action to the words.

Later, Tom gave them all a full account of the trail-blazing space voyage. They were amazed to learn about the uncharted moonlet.

"Thank goodness there aren't any more of them," Sandy said.

Mr. Swift, who was flying back to Shopton, promised to phone Mr. Bruce and the other network men as soon as he reached home. Late the next day, he radioed Tom that the broadcasters had agreed to the new location above Loonaui for the space station.

"Now we're all set!" Tom said exultantly, thumping Bud on the back.

"You mean the expedition can get under way?"

"As soon as the rockets are ready for take-off!"

During the next few days, cargo jets shuttled back and forth from Shopton to Loonaui on a stepped-up schedule. By the end of the week, the entire space crew of almost fifty men had arrived on the island. Among them was Chow Winkler.

"Brand my neutralator, you got a reg'lar rocket city built up on this little ole island!" He gaped at the vast extent of the humming base, with its miles of machine shops, commissary, barracks, and recreation areas. Special docks had been built for the fuel tankers and salvage tugs. And the hangars and warehouses were crammed with supplies and parts assemblies for the outpost in space.

The start of the expedition was set for the following morning. Amid great fanfare, part of the first section of the giant space wheel was blasted aloft in an unmanned cargo rocket. The rest of the great central hub was sent up shortly after lunch.

"Who's gonna ride herd on them contraptions?" puzzled Chow, as the second rocket streaked upward.

"No one," explained Tom. "Once they reach the orbit, they'll just float around up there till the space crews arrive to unload them."

Chow scratched his chin and shook his head uneasily. "I still don't see what's gonna keep things in place up there. But I reckon there ain't much you could use fer a hitchin' post at that!"

The crew spent the rest of the afternoon going over the operation of the tiny one-man rockets which they would use for their construction work in space. Motive power was supplied by swivel-mounted reaction pistols in back, fired by triggers inside the rocket.

"And remember," Bud warned them grimly, "keep these babies attached to your mother ship by a cable at all times. Otherwise you may blast yourselves off into eternity!"

Before supper, Tom made the announcement for which everyone was waiting. "Launching of the manned rockets begins tomorrow morning. Number One will blast off at eight o'clock, with Ken Horton in charge. The other rockets will follow at twelve-hour intervals."

News of the coming take-offs electrified the camp. The crewmen were keyed to a high pitch of anticipation. Horton and his crew would be in a rocket containing one of the broadcasting sections.

As eight o'clock approached, Tom entered the pilot's cabin with the crew and checked the flight tape. Then he shook hands all around, adding:

"This is a big moment for all of us. You're leaving on one of the greatest voyages in human history. Good luck and we'll join you soon!"

Blast-off proceeded smoothly. Tom stayed with the radar-tracking crew, exchanging signals with the rocket until it reached the orbit safely about one o'clock that afternoon.

At eight that evening, rocket Number Two took off, with Hank Sterling in charge. It contained the crew's bunkroom section of the wheel.

Next day, two more rockets were launched on the same time schedule—one at eight A.M., the other at eight P.M. The first was the mess hall and recreation spoke of the space wheel; the other, the observatory in which the telescope would be mounted.

"I see you have us posted, Tom, to leave tomorrow on Number Five," Bud remarked, as the smoke cleared from the launching area.

Tom nodded. "From here on, the launchings will go like clockwork. We'll be a lot more useful on the construction job up in the orbit."

Chow, who was standing nearby, broke in, "You got *me* down fer Number Seven!"

"That's right. You'll take off Friday morning."

The weather-beaten face of the roly-poly chef had an aggrieved look. "Why, brand my radarscope, you wouldn't send me up with someone else, would you, Tom? Only reason I'm leavin' this little ole earth is so I can stick with you!"

Tom could not resist Chow's plea. "Okay." He laughed. "You can fly in our rocket. But be ready to take off at eight tomorrow morning."

Chow said with a wide smile, "Now you're talkin', Tom! I'll go pack my pans right now!"

Tom stayed in the blockhouse for a while, listening to the radio reports from rocket Number Four. Then he strolled back through the darkness to his cottage. Bud was getting ready to turn in.

"What's wrong?" he asked, noting the troubled look on Tom's face.

"It's the Gorilla, I guess. I can't help worrying that he may try something after we take off."

Bud laid a hand on his friend's shoulder. "Relax, spaceboy. The way this island's guarded, even a seagull couldn't sneak in without being spotted."

Tom shrugged. "Maybe so, but I still wish that man was behind bars." The young inventor paused, his brow puckered in thought. "Bud, suppose you were Blatka and wanted to attack Loonaui. How would you try to get past the island's defenses?"

"He can't—that's just what I'm telling you," Bud insisted. "We have planes, ships, and radar on guard against a sneak raid, so how could—"

"Wait a second!" Tom jumped up from his chair excitedly. "That's it! We have planes, ships, and radar, *but no defense against underwater attack!*"

"Huh?" Bud's mouth dropped open.

"Hop into your clothes! We have a job to do!"

A few moments later the boys piled into their jeep and sped to the security shack. Tom rapped out orders to Ames and Radnor:

"Call Dilling from the blockhouse and round up every electronics man who's not on duty!"

While this was being done, Tom hastily sketched out the circuit diagrams for a makeshift sonar set. The detection device would beam out ultrasonic pulses underwater and pick up any echoes both on headphones and on a cathode-ray scope.

Tom handed the drawings to Dilling. "Have your men rig up half a dozen of these sets pronto! I want them planted all around the island!"

By midnight the sonar sets were ready and crews were putting them into action at six different points around the shore line. They would sweep the entire underwater approaches to Loonaui.

Tom and Bud waited tensely in the security shack. Within an hour the first walkie-talkie call came in. "Reporting from Coral Point. We've picked up a submarine moving into the cove!"

Their hearts thumping, the boys drove to the scene by jeep with Ames and Radnor. When they arrived, the submarine's propellers could no longer be heard over the earphones, indicating that the engines had been stopped. But the submarine itself still showed plainly on the scope.

"It must be going to surface and send raiders ashore," commented Bud.

"We'd better take cover and be ready to nab them as soon as they set foot on the beach," suggested Ames.

They took cover in a grove of palms surrounded by thick bushes. As they waited, the silence of the moonlit night was broken only by the faint drone of planes circling the island and the ruffle of the surf against the beach.

Twenty minutes went by, then half an hour. A check with the sonar set showed that the submarine was still resting on the bottom.

Phil Radnor was puzzled. "What's their game?"

Tom's voice was grim and tense as he replied, "There's only one answer. Loonaui is volcanic—it's made of soft lava rock. They must be planting bombs underwater to blow up the island!"

CHAPTER 24

UNDERWATER DANGER

TOM'S WORDS sent a chill of fear through his listeners. A few well-placed demolition bombs could blast the tiny island into a shambles!

"Bud, we'll get into diving suits pronto and go down to that sub!" Tom urged. "Are you with me?"

"Sure. But what's the pitch?"

"We'll foul their propellers with chains till we find out who they are. If they're Blatka's men, we'll make them disarm the bombs!"

"You're on!"

Tom barked orders over the short wave and a few minutes later a salvage tug arrived from a nearby dock. Tom and Bud donned diving suits and helmets, and slipped into the moonlit, phosphorescent waters of the cove, carrying the chains.

Like a grim and deadly shark waiting for prey, the submarine lay motionless on the bottom. Working swiftly, the boys wove the heavy chains around her twin screws. Then Tom pulled a wrench from his belt and tapped on the submarine's hull in international code:

"Who are you?"

He pressed his helmet against the side of the submarine, but there was no reply. Tom repeated the signal. Again, he got no response. So he tapped out a new message:

"This is Tom Swift. We have fouled your propellers, so you can't get away. You have no choice but to identify yourself."

This time, when Tom pressed his helmet against the hull, the submarine began to vibrate. Its motors were being started! A moment later the craft shuddered violently. Its propeller blades snapped and curled as the chains held them fast.

The boys looked at each other, wondering what would happen next. Finally a blast of air churned the water as the submarine began to rise from the depths.

The boys signaled to be brought up. By the time they climbed aboard the tug, the submarine had surfaced. Searchlights from the tug pinned her conning tower in a blinding, relentless glare.

A hatch opened and men began to tumble out, blinking and shielding their eyes. In the lead was a hulking, brutish figure.

"The Gorilla!" exclaimed Bud.

At a sharp command from Harlan Ames, the prisoners clambered aboard the tug which had edged alongside. To everyone's amazement, they were in no mood for a fight. Instead, they were trembling with fear.

"Quick! There is no time to lose!" Blatka shouted in a heavily accented voice. "We have planted a bomb! It will explode in less than an hour!"

There was no doubt that he spoke the truth. His companions looked at Tom with terrified eyes.

Tom said quickly, "The bomb must be disarmed at once! Where is it?"

Blatka offered to go down with Tom. But Ames and Bud were afraid that he might try to attack the young inventor underwater. They insisted that others go down with them. This meant a delay while more diving equipment was brought.

Time was growing short as Tom, Blatka, Bud, and another diver donned the suits and went over the side. They plodded their way through the shadowy depths to the point where the bomb had been planted in the soft lava-rock wall of the island. With the Gorilla's assistance, Tom quickly unscrewed the fuse.

"Wow!" Bud gasped as the air-pump man lifted off his helmet a few minutes later. "The way my heart was thumping down there, I was afraid I might *jar* that bomb into exploding!"

With the danger past, Blatka and his men lapsed into gloomy apathy. Like all fanatics, the wreckage of their plans plunged them into despair. Under Ames' prodding, they talked freely but sullenly.

"We are members of a secret society," mumbled

Blatka. "Our mission was to destroy all the top scientists in America. Now that we have failed, our lives are worthless. Even in our own country, nothing awaits us but a firing squad!"

The Gorilla admitted that his group had fired the guided missile at the *Sky Queen* and dropped the bomb off Fearing Island. He and another man had knocked out Tom and Bud in Shopton, but had been scared off by an approaching car. The tank of nerve gas sent to Tom's laboratory was also the work of Blatka's gang. They, too, had launched the midnight projectile which overshot Loonaui Island.

"From now on, you'll do all your bombing on a rock pile!" Ames told the men grimly.

When the tug docked, Ames and Radnor turned their prisoners over to the island police.

"What a night!" said Bud, as he and Tom drove back to their cottage. "I'm glad your mother and the girls didn't know about it."

"Same here, Bud."

In the morning Mrs. Swift, Sandy, and Phyl were on hand for the next launching, and Mr. Swift and Uncle Ned arrived at the last moment to watch it. All wished the group Godspeed.

With Tom, Bud, Chow, and another crewman strapped to their couches in the flight compartment, the ship blasted off into the blue. Like the other rockets designed for this project, it dropped off only two stages en route. The third stage, which was hauled clear up to the orbit, would come apart in three sections. The center would become one of the spokes of the space wheel. The nose and firing engines would be coupled together and would be used to ferry spacemen back to Loonaui whenever that became desirable.

The trip skyward went smoothly. When they arrived at the rendezvous, 22,300 miles above Loonaui, the travelers stared out of the transparent pilot's canopy.

"Brand my headphones," gasped Chow, "I sure never seen nothin' like this back in Texas!"

An awesome sight met their eyes. In the starry blackness of outer space floated a great silver wheel hub, with huge holes where the twelve spokes would be connected. Ranged around it were the first four rocket ships. Swarming all about were tiny space-suited figures and midget construction rockets, tied to their mother craft by long lines. Working with cables and winches, the men were trying to maneuver the rocket ships into their hub holes.

Tom tuned his rocket radio to the right frequency for local communication and spoke into the mike. "Calling all crew captains. Can you hear me?" One by one, they reported. "I'm glad to see the wheel hub's all erected," Tom said.

"Yes, but these spokes are giving us plenty of headaches," replied Hank Sterling.

"We've been working on them in shifts for the past twelve hours," added Ken Horton, "and we don't have even one connected."

"Want us to pile out and help?" Tom asked.

"Not yet. Get your own rocket into place first."

It soon became clear to Tom that Hank and Ken had not exaggerated the difficulties of the job. The powerful blasts of the steering motors made it hard to jockey the ship at close quarters. Again and again, Tom nosed the ship toward its berth, only to wind up out of line, or aimed at the wrong angle. Once he swung clear around broadside to the hub.

"Whew!" he gasped. "This is worse than any target I've ever tried to hit!"

But finally Tom's skill and experience on past rocket flights turned the trick.

"You're in, pal!" Bud exulted.

"Nice work, skipper," radioed Hank Sterling. "But what's your secret?"

"Give us time to eat and rest up a bit and we'll show you how it's done," replied Tom, chuckling.

The next step was to weld the spoke in place. The nose section was then unscrewed and wormed back through the hollow spoke. A crew outside in space suits then sent it off to a distance of a hundred feet to await further use as a ferry to Loonaui.

Before long the construction job was progressing rapidly. One by one, the other wheel spokes were connected. As fresh rockets arrived in the orbit, they too were coupled to the hub. Then work on equipping the various laboratories and factories was begun.

"Just one more spoke to go," remarked Bud one

day, as he and Tom stood chained to the top of one of the solar-battery sections. In the eerie silence their riveting tools gave off not the slightest sound.

Through the glass port of his helmet, Tom's face looked worried. "That last rocket's way overdue, Bud," he radioed back. "Let's go inside and check."

Dilling reported from Loonaui that Number Twelve had not been heard from since two hours after blast-off. The crew captain was Arvid Hanson.

After trying unsuccessfully to make radio contact with the missing ship, Tom said, "I'm going to look for it!"

He and Bud took off in one of the empty cargo rockets. Tom steered a course earthward.

Suddenly Bud pointed to the radarscope with a shout. "There it is!"

Using the portable reaction pistols to propel them-

Maneuvering carefully with his steering jets, Tom sped toward the object shown on the scope. "Calling rocket Number Twelve! . . . Can you hear me, Arv? . . . Come in, please!"

Still there was no reply. Gradually the missing rocket came into view. Dreading what he and Bud might find, Tom overtook it and steered alongside.

To his relief, the crewmen were grouped under the canopy, alive and safe!

Using his arms as signal flags, Hanson semaphored, "Our flight tape jammed. We're out of fuel and our radio's dead!"

selves, they unreeled a hose from the fuel ship

"Thank goodness you're alive," Tom replied. "I'll have the base send up a fuel rocket."

Anxious hours went by as they waited for the fuel ship. Finally it came hurtling into view and nudged into orbital flight directly above them. Tom and Bud donned their space suits. Then, using the portable reaction pistols strapped to their backs to propel themselves, they unreeled a hose from the fuel ship down to rocket Number Twelve.

An hour later Hanson's rocket and Tom's headed upward to the space station. Tom jockeyed Number Twelve into place and the men entered the hub.

"Say, where's everybody?" Bud asked. The hub was usually alive with workers.

Tom looked into the next laboratory. No one was there. Disturbed, he and the others peered into one room after another. At last they found all the crew in the bunk section. Sound asleep, they lay in grotesque positions on beds and benches.

"Good night!" Bud exclaimed. "What's wrong with these guys?"

With a sinking heart Tom replied, "I'm afraid that it's space sickness, due to the lack of gravity. Until now it hadn't affected—"

The inventor's words died away as a terrific impact hit the space station.

"Hey, what's going on?" Bud cried out.

The space wheel began to spin crazily. Tom and his friends, thrown violently off their feet, blacked out!

CHAPTER 25

OUTPOST IN THE SKY

AS THE GREAT silver sky wheel whirled around, the unconscious crewmen were flung to the outer end of the bunkroom compartment by centrifugal force.

They lay huddled and helpless. But at last Tom stirred and raised his head. Then Chow and Arv Hanson showed signs of regaining consciousness. Gradually the others began to revive.

"Good night! What hit us?" Bud murmured.

"I don't know," Tom replied, struggling to his feet. "But we'd better stop this crate from spinning before everything is ruined!"

Scrambling wildly, he made his way toward the storage hold in the central hub and grabbed a dozen powdered rockets used for harpooning lines from one point to another, and also two reaction pistols. He kept one and handed the other to Ken Horton.

"Ken, you and Hank put on your space suits and climb out through the air hatch at the far end of the bunkroom compartment. Bud and I will do the same on the other side of the wheel. Then start firing your pistol in the same direction we're spinning!" Tom added an urgent reminder to hook on their safety lines before opening the hatch.

"Righto, skipper!"

The boys donned their own space gear, then clambered out through the air lock of the hospital spoke. In the black void all around them, the stars seemed to be sweeping past at merry-go-round speed.

Clinging perilously to the handrails outside the hatch, Tom and Bud managed to brace themselves while they attached the rockets to the rim. Then, holding their reaction pistols, they triggered off a series of short bursts. At the same instant, the powdered rockets burst into action. Communicating via the radio sets inside their helmets, the boys timed their fire with that of Ken and Hank on the opposite side of the wheel. Gradually the whirling space station slowed to a halt from the braking effect of the pistol blasts.

Climbing back inside the wheel, the boys returned to the bunkhouse and removed their space suits. Suddenly Bud stared at the crewmen, then exclaimed in amazement:

"Say! You fellows aren't dopey any more! Not even our doctor."

Young Dr. Blaine grinned. "That supposed to be a compliment?"

"No, I'm serious." Bud explained how he and the others had arrived at the space wheel to find the whole crew limp and dazed.

The men received this news in puzzled surprise. "Is that true, Tom, or is Bud kidding?"

"No, he's not, but whatever hit the space station must have jarred you all back to your senses."

Dr. Blaine smiled. "Maybe that's the right medicine when someone gets space happy up here—give him some kind of a jolt."

"I believe that you're right," said Tom thoughtfully. "The time element was one thing I didn't reckon with." Smiling wanly, he added, "Perhaps frequent vacations back on earth will be the answer. And now, let's find out what hit us and check the damage."

Before starting his inspection of the space wheel, Tom instructed his crew captains to assemble their men for a roll call. He wanted to make sure that none of the men had been injured or lost in the accident. To his dismay, Bob Jeffers and another young mechanic were missing!

Tom rapped out orders to his crew chiefs:

"Search your own rocket section—the one you brought up to the orbit. Then report to me in the hub."

Several tense minutes passed, but finally a crew

captain came hurrying back with word that Jeffers and his companion were in a broadcasting compartment. They had been knocked out by the sudden crash and were just now coming to.

"Better take them to sick bay and have Doc look at them."

Just then, another crew chief came in. "Tom, something hit your lab!"

He explained that when he had stepped into the air lock leading to the laboratory section, the warning alarm had started buzzing. The red signal light had flashed. As he looked through the quartz-glass window of the inside door, the man had seen why. The outside end of the laboratory had been sheared off, and all the air had leaked out of the compartment.

Once again, Tom and Bud donned their space suits and went to investigate. Besides the damage from the crash, which had wrecked some of Tom's precious scientific equipment, there were also charred and blackened areas caused by burning. But the fire had evidently gone out quickly, due to the metallic materials and the loss of air.

"What caused it? A meteor?" Bud asked.

The young inventor nodded glumly. "No doubt about it. That's what started the space station spinning, too." Tom looked around at the shambles and heaved a deep sigh. "Oh, well, I guess we're lucky that it didn't hit the bunkroom, or we all would be dead."

"Cheer up, inventor boy," said Bud sympathetically. "We can soon repair this place."

Tom responded with a grin, "Good advice, Bud.
Let's get busy!"

With the crew working in round-the-clock shifts
again, the sheared-off laboratory section was rebuilt
in three days. A special cargo rocket was sent up
from Loonaui with tanks of oxygen and helium to
restore the air mixture.

A week later the first groups of technical men arrived to begin work, including biologists, astronomers, broadcasting engineers, and medical men.

"Brand my space suit, this little ole space hive is
buzzin' more'n a bee's nest in Texas!" remarked
Chow, as he watched a newly arrived rocket ship discharge its passengers. And he added with a chuckle,
"My galley ain't the best place in the world fer
cookin', but it sure feeds a lot o' hungry folks. They
got as big appetites up here as any place!"

The great silver station was now a more imposing
sight than ever. Besides the latticework telescope
poking out from the astronomer's observatory, the
wheel also bristled with radar scanners, and radio
and TV antennae. From the factory sections, wedge-
shaped lids opened up, revealing polished mirrors
to catch and reflect the sun's rays in toward the solar-
battery assembly line.

A few days later Tom looked up from his desk as
Bud came into his laboratory compartment through
the air lock.

"Know how long we've been up here?" he asked.

"Fresh out of calendars, Tom."

"Thirty days. A pretty long stretch living without gravity. The replacement crew is on its way up here now, so we can head for a vacation back on earth."

"*Yippee!*" Bud let out a whoop and went off to spread the news.

When their rocket landed on Loonaui, the island went wild with excitement. And an even greater thrill was in store the next day when Tom and Bud reached San Francisco. Both families and Phyl and her father greeted them excitedly with handclasps, hugs, kisses, and congratulations.

Police battled to keep back the cheering, flag-waving crowds who turned out to do honor to the inventor of the first outpost in space. Reporters who crowded around wanted to know what Tom's next invention would be.

"I honestly don't know," he replied. As it happened, a newsman later titled the story *Tom Swift and His Diving Seacopter*.

Tom was asked for a statement as newsreel and television cameras took pictures. Smiling, he glanced skyward for a moment, then said, "Next visit up there, I'm going to head for a satellite of Mars. But right now—you can quote me on this—it's good to be back on the planet Earth!"